Also by Olga Bogdan:

HELENA

OLGA BOGDAN

Igor

Wrong Place Wrong Time

ttt

Published by TruerThanTruth Production 2018
www.truerthantruth.com

© Olga Bogdan 2018

Cover design by Tim Peplow
tim@pepco.co.uk

Interior design by Polgarus Studio
polgarusstudio.com

For all enquiries, please contact:
info@truerthantruth.com
info@olgabogdan.com

This is a work of fiction. Names, characters, businesses,
places, events and incidents are either the products of the
author's imagination or used in a fictitious manner. Any
resemblance to actual persons, living or dead, or actual
events is purely coincidental.

IGOR

ISBN 978-1-9998043-2-9 (paperback)
ISBN 978-1-9998043-3-6 (e-book)

With special thanks to Helen Baggott and Valentina Djordjević.

CONTENTS

IGOR

PROLOGUE

Mema liked nothing better than chew on a bit of gristle. She didn't care where her nourishment came from, chicken's foot, pig's ear or ox's tail, as long as it came attached to bone and sinew. It was the connective tissue between the more banal parts of a beast that really impressed her. She frowned upon things like sirloin steak and double-glazed ham. She would rather starve to death than be seen eating the boring straightforward pieces of flesh. 'Who do you think I am?' She would say to an unsuspecting waiter or a kindly host keen to impress by offering the finest, juiciest, most tender cuts of meat. 'A barbarian?' No: all you needed to do to keep Mema entertained was give her the gnarliest, ugliest bone of them all, with plenty of cartilage and ligaments knotted around it, then wait for the sound of the happy crunching to commence.

'Hey, Mema!' I once called over to the grown-up dining table. 'A great white wouldn't stand a chance with you, you'd eat her in 1-2-3, wouldn't you, Mema? Wouldn't you?'

'I don't know.' With a precision of a master bricklayer, Mema heaped bone marrow on top of a small crust of bread, smoothed it over with a butter knife, then sprinkled the mixture of a freshly grated horseradish and sea salt on top. 'Has it got any gristle?'

'It's *all* gristle, Mema!' I screeched. 'We studied sharks in science last week, and dolphins too! Would you eat a dolphin then, Mema? Would you eat a lovely dolphin, eh greedy girl?'

'Stop shouting, you little hooligan!' my dad said. 'And let your grannie eat in peace.

JUST DESERTS

I knew the crunching sound meant Bella's nose was broken. I tried not to look at her, not see, but then I went and turned my head anyway, and I saw her face, saw it wasn't her face any more, and I opened my mouth to scream but of course that ship had sailed a long time ago. Guess Bella screamed for both of us, she was always a nice girl, giving; besides, she had every reason to scream, she had every reason to let it all out, she had every right. The man who attacked her, the dark newcomer, vicious as an old nettle bush and at least fifty times as angry, he meant to hurt her. He was all about hurting people, especially the little pretty defenceless ones, like Bella. The minute I saw him walking towards our cage, I knew this was not the usual social call. Other men, they were cocky on the outside, but inside they squirmed with guilt, as well as fear that they may end up in hell for what they were about to do. This man, the newcomer, he was a rare breed. A motherless child, godless child, didn't think twice before unleashing his demons upon the world. No shame to hold him back, no power. There was nothing stopping him, and in Bella's case not even the usual need to look after the merchandise.

His eyes shone black, the colour of his dark bastard soul, and then they switched off completely.

I don't know how I know about things. I just do, I just happen to know stuff about stuff. A cross for me to bear for sure, in particular when it comes to my mind-blowing talent for spotting evil. As talents go, looks like I drew a short straw yet again, because what's the point in clocking a shitstorm charging at you at fifty million miles per hour, I mean it's not like you come equipped with an umbrella that's capable of withstanding such force. No such thing exists, unless the Japanese have invented it whilst I was busy looking the other way, namely towards this epic shitstorm that by the way keeps following me no matter where I go. Nothing I can do about that, except sit there, waiting to be hit.

Well not this time, not with Bella next to me, not when I'm probably going to be next anyway. I start rattling the bars, jumping up and down like a circus flea, kicking the lock until my feet bleed, not because I think this would change anything, but because I want to have my last say in this world, even if I no longer have the voice to express it.

Darkness comes quickly. I am very lucky like that, no matter what else is happening in my world, I can always count on passing out when things get too unpleasant for my own personal taste. A bit like an antelope, blacking-out moments before a lion sinks his teeth into its neck. I used to watch *Survival* a lot, that's how I know. Never thought it would come in useful, but I guess Mema was right when she said I made a very good mimic.

Passing out is not to be confused with the girlie act of fainting. That's something entirely different, because, unlike most girls, I'm not asking to be rescued, or asking for a pardon: I'm simply removing myself from the unsympathetic environment. I'd never ever beg for my so-called life, not in a million years; I'd much rather get eaten, get it done and over with; bye-bye cruel world and good bloody riddance.

Except that sometimes you don't get eaten. The lion kind of loses interest and leaves you laying on the ground, three-quarter dead, bits of you strewn here, there and everywhere, each one hurting like hell spelt backwards.

Not talking about myself here, for a change, I'm talking about Bella.

'Pull her out!' I open my eyes before it's safe to do so, and manage to just about catch the expression of flat terror on Bella's face, as her head clanks out after the rest of the body. Panting, I pull myself up on all fours. Something pokes into the palm of my left hand. It's a tooth. I run my tongue over my own personal set. All there, bar the big one at the back I lost to eating too many sugar cubes. Mema said so, and she wagged her finger at me, but still I refused to eat the gristle.

'What if I paid you?' she said. 'In gold coins?'

I sighed. 'Not even then.'

'And how about the fat around the ham?'

I really wanted those gold coins, because I was saving up to buy a lovely big white horse then ride it up and down my street and watch everyone go green with envy. But I still said no.

'Come on, just a sliver. No man would ever marry a girl with a scrawny backside!'

'No, Mema, no I said! And I will never get married, so why would I care what some stupid man thinks of me?'

I slip the tooth in my shorts pocket. The heat inside the back of the truck is crushing the life out of me in an unbearably slow motion. Whatever's out there must be better than this hellhole. I slip out of the truck like a giant slimy slug, hit the ground with a thud.

I was wrong.

'And who the fuck's this?'

How rude. If I were in a fit state to make a run for it, this would've been my final clue. But I'm not. Never been what you'd call a runner, more of a light a fag wait for another bus type. I spot Bella's naked body twitch about in the yellow dust marbled with orange streaks of blood, and my mind goes blank for like a second. The next second, I'm wishing that Bella's no longer in there, that she's had enough sense to leave behind this messed-up body writhing around in the bloody mud, and is now soaring free, way high up in the pale blue sky, like an eagle or something. 'Leave well alone,' Mema used to tell me whenever she caught me picking my nose, or spots or any other part of my anatomy. And, 'Walk in the opposite direction,' whenever I got too close to the tray of buttery lemon biscuits fresh out of the oven. 'You'll only burn your fingers.' But I never listened, I only pretended to. So instead of making my wish then pouring myself a large scotch and go sit in a hammock or something, I run over to Bella, give her shoulder a little nudge. She looks up. Her mouth is wide open, but no sound comes out. I open my mouth, but no sound comes out. This is so horrible that even I realize that I should've left well alone. Should've nailed my feet to the ground. I turn to run, fuck the next bus, but someone grabs me around the waist and lifts me off the ground.

'Play dead,' the voice whispers. 'Or get dead.'

I look up at my captor and immediately give up the struggle. Another recent arrival to the Camp Shithole, this man is light not dark, and I'm not only saying this because his eyes are the colour of the underside of an angel's wing, his hair is soft and blond and basically dead sexy, and he smells of something I'd like to eat. Can't think of what it is right now. Strange that, as I tend to do my best so-called thinking when under unnecessary pressure.

'I said, what's up with the runt?' The tallest man I have ever lived to see walks over and lifts my chin by a single flick of his abnormally long forefinger. 'Hm. Dirty girl, aren't you? And not in a good way.'

'This is the girl I was telling you about, Boss, the one who hit Rob over the head,' says a voice to my left. It belongs to Miki, the man who chucked me into the truck after I've smashed that brick over the dark newcomer's head. 'Count your lucky stars, girl,' he told me. 'Whatever waits for you on the other side has got to be better than what Rob will do to you after he comes around.' He then paused for what seemed like an unnecessary waste of a lifetime. 'How old are you?' His little brown eyes, the colour of toasted shit, bore into me like a couple of rusty nails. I was just starting to suspect the poor man must be in love with me or something, when he went and spoilt it all by saying, 'Too old. And sick in the head. Women like you should be drowned at birth.' Not a very nice thing to say to a girl with so much to live for, is it now. 'Got him good, too, he was still out when we left.'

'This little one?' The giant stares at me. 'You floored Rob?'

'She doesn't speak, Boss,' says Blondie. 'Never did.'

'A mute whore? I like the sound of that,' says Boss. 'Is she any good? Jett?'

I look at Bella. Wonder what will happen to her next. Wonder why she didn't go down, like an antelope. Stupid Bella. Stupid me, for never thinking of teaching her.

'I haven't had a chance to sample, Boss,' says the man holding me. Jett, is it. Not ideal, but better than Blondie I suppose. 'Not yet.'

Boss finally lets go of my chin, then looks around. 'Well? Anyone?'

A bearded man to my left goes first. 'Well, Boss, I haven't personally sampled her as such, but that's only because I thought she was Miki's.'

'No way she's mine!' says Miki.

'I swear on my mother's grave you said you liked her,' says Beard. 'I heard you say you liked the little one. So I kept myself to myself.'

'Is that how you got crabs?' Jett still has me by the scruff of the neck, but gently, like I was his cat or something. 'By keeping yourself to yourself, you dirty mother fucker?'

'Hey!' Beard looks hurt. 'That was a confidential information that was!'

Everyone laughs. Except for Boss. I get that. Bosses can only laugh at comedies which they must watch behind closed door in the privacy of their own home. Otherwise their men will see them as soft and shoot them down at the first opportunity. Sometimes they'll allow themselves a wry smile when looking at a small child, or a pair of kittens, fooling around. But that's all. I saw enough gangster movies and also westerns to know all of the above to be a fact.

'Pardon my French well in advance, but are you telling me no one's fucked her?' says Boss. 'Eh? What did I tell you about un-sampled goods?'

'I know this one!' And the eager beaver award goes to Beard. 'Un-sampled goods are like a tickling bomb.'

'A *ticking* bomb,' says Boss. 'You moron.'

'Oh,' says Beard. 'It makes far more sense now.'

'Every ticking bomb has a potential to go off,' recites Boss. 'Taking with it our property and most likely our lives. That's why I asked you – no, why I *ordered* you to sample each and every whore. We need to ensure there's no ticking left in her before we send her out into the world to earn our living.'

'When I said I liked the little one,' says Miki, 'I must've been talking about Nico. Or Sam. This one, she sort of slipped below my radar.'

'Slipped, did she?' Boss throws his arms in the air, like a proper drama queen with a spider complex. 'Anyone else?'

His men look at one another.

'I thought you did.'

'I was sure she was yours.'

'Mine? I thought she went with young Blake.'

'Blake? He doesn't even like pussy!'

'You don't say!'

'Shut up!' Howls Boss. 'Useless, the lot of you!' He then walks over to Bella, gives her side a little kick. 'That animal! I said half-alive, not half-dead! Right, round up the rest of the whores!'

Miki runs over to the truck parked just off a dusty trail, and lifts off the canvas. 'Out, you bitches, and don't you make me say it twice!' He spits on the ground as the first whore wobbles off the truck, blinded by the sun, patent white stilettoes tucked under her arm for safe-keeping. The second one, platinum bombshell with the biggest bazookas I've ever poked my eye on, teeters out in come-hither red leather boots riding all the way up to her mid-thigh. But hey, what's Miki up to, that hilarious old joker. Oh wait, he's sticking out his foot for the whore to trip over, and like a silly goose that's exactly what she does next. So now we have a whore lying face down in the dirt, and the men hollering with delight. Has my life really come to this. She tries to get up, but Miki pushes her back down with his highly polished black and white brogue. He poses like a hunter triumphing over his prey. 'Anyone got a camera?'

'Cut it out, Miki! We don't have all day,' says Boss. 'Let's get this party over and done with, I'm a busy fucking businessman with an important *business* to attend to, you ignorant bunch of village monkeys!'

Miki lets Bombshell go; she takes a bow before swaying off after the first girl, like she owns the situation, although it is clear to me that she bloody well doesn't. The next whore to get off is black, and sort of small and bony like a baby chick, with hair to match. Miki offers her his hand, but pulls it away just as she's about to grab it. 'Oh look at this bitch here, wants my hand of marriage, she does! The only hand you'll be getting from me is–'

'Where's my shotgun?' asks Boss. 'Let's see if he can make jokes with his balls shot off.'

'Alright, Boss, alright…' Miki hustles out the rest of the girls. 'Out you get, move on, and stop looking so scared, you look ten times uglier when you're scared; smile, bitches, smile!'

'Bring them out,' says Boss. I can feel Jett's hand on the back of my neck tighten ever so slightly. A couple of men run off, and all too soon return, each struggling to keep a huge dog at the end of a thick shiny chain. I don't know what sort of pooches these are, never seen anything like it before in my life, not even on *Survival*. So naturally I name them Hellhound I and Hellhound II, not because I lack in imagination, but because this is what hellhounds must look like, and if they don't, then they really truly ought to try. Boss turns to face the women. 'Okay, ladies, what you're about to witness here is the very last scene in a play about betrayal, dishonesty and downright unfaithfulness. I could go on about it some distance, but like I said, I'm a busy man with an important business to run, so let's keep it short and

11

sweet, eh? You all know Bella, you all know what she did, and now you're about to learn what happens to people who deceive me. Ay. Guys, without any further ado – release the hounds!'

I yelp. I don't know why, but I do. It's like a big hiccough coming out of me, or some sort of a spasm. Couldn't be helped. Boss holds up his hand. I yelp again. He looks at what's left of Bella, then back at me.

'The runt,' he says. 'It's making noises.'

'She does that, sometimes,' says Miki. 'I think she must be retarded, you know, not quite right in her head.'

'I know what retarded means,' says Boss. 'She surprised me, that's all.'

'What do you want us to do with her?' asks Miki. 'Eh Boss? What shall we do with the runt?'

Boss this, Boss that. What an ass-lick.

'She can join the rest of the troupe,' Jett shoves me toward the whores. 'Go on, fuck off!'

'Or maybe we should strip her naked, cover her in honey and tie her up to a tree as an offering for the Hill People?' Miki grabs my arm, pulls me close. I notice Jett flinch. What's wrong with Jett. Why can't he just relax and enjoy the fun day out with the boys. 'Or she could always join her friend.' My vote's with the Hill People. 'Eh Boss?' Miki's fingers dig into my flesh like talons. I feel like crying but instead I make myself a promise that I shall never rest until Miki pays for all the bad things he has ever done, first and foremost for calling me a retard. I will haunt him until he begs for forgiveness, and then I will haunt him some more and then I will kill him. I give myself an imaginary high-five, and almost feel sorry for Miki, for his destiny's just been sealed, and not in a good way, not for him at least. 'Rob didn't exactly leave much flesh on that bone, and the dogs, Boss, they're ravenous…'

Boss shrugs. 'If no one wants to fuck her, she's useless to me.'

'She could work in the kitchen!' Jett goes to pull me back, but quick as a flash, Miki swings me around to his left, out of Jett's reach. I catch a spark of malice in Miki's eyes and realise that this must be personal. Not that I care what score these two pimping bastards have got to settle, I just sort of really wish Jett won. Or starts winning any time soon. 'Or help clean the joint.'

Christ. Jett must really be into me. Yeah. That must be it.

Boss stands there for a moment, his lips pursed, his hands resting across the middle of his chest. 'We already have a cleaner. Throw her to the lions!'

What happened next is hard for me to describe. I was there, but I guess I must've gone into an antelope trance of sorts. All I know is this: Miki grabbed my arm and made me sit in the orange dirt. I caught a glimpse of one girl with tears in her eyes, and another grinning like a Cheshire cat on double-acid; I saw Jett's face turn to stone, I saw Beard pulling on his beard, and I heard a bird cry, lost his way home some place high up in the sky was my guess.

When the Hellhounds got unleashed, Hellhound I went straight for Bella, and started to shred her body into bloody ribbons. Hellhound II hesitated, before bounding towards me. I stared at his muscles flexing at the front of his chest, splattered by the foam that escaped from his mouth, until all I could see were his teeth, white and glistening like an army of ghosts. I yelped. Hellhound II stopped dead in his tracks, his face less than a centimetre away from mine. I yelped again. Hellhound II sniffed my ear. I started to growl. He growled back. I growled louder. He backed off and disappeared into the bushes, only to suddenly reappear and, faster than lightning strikes, sink his teeth into Boss's waist.

I would like to say that this is the point where things turned real nasty, except that they already had, and a long, long time ago at that. The women were screaming, the men were shouting, aiming their guns and rifles at Hellhound II before thinking twice about accidentally shooting Boss, and holding back. I got on all fours, growling and soaking up Bella's blood because the earth has had its fill, and then a thought flashed through my head. 'Enough!' I pounced at Hellhound I, who was still snapping at the loose flesh and mud, and I sank my teeth into his neck, locking my jaw deep inside his mother fucking murdering neck until I heard the familiar sound of gristle crunching which is when I let go and went for Hellhound II.

PEARL

I dot the dough with butter and sprinkle it with a little semolina.

'Too much butter!' Lwalida slaps the back of my leg. 'Too little semolina! The *msemen* will stick, and you father will not eat it. Waste!'

'Isra! Oh Isra!' our neighbour Zayna calls out of her kitchen window. 'Can you give me a hand with my washing? My back is stiff and achy.'

'I will, Zayna, I will!' Lwalida hurries off outside, dragging her fat bottom behind. 'I was trying to teach my lazy and extravagant daughter how to cook! Why did Allah think I would prosper from having seven useless daughters is a mystery to me.'

'*Alahu Akbar,*' replies Zayna.

'*Alhamdulillah,*' says Lwalida.

I give the sore spot on my leg a quick rub, before adding another pinch of semolina, and folding the sides of the dough into the centre until I have a neat square. The skillet is smoking hot and ready. Lwalida is lying. I always make good *msemen*, and this time it won't be any different. Father will eat at least four, he never eats less than four *msemen* before his lunch and he licks his fingers after each one.

'Amina, Amina!' Two of my youngest sisters run into the kitchen. 'We're hungry!'

I step in front of the skillet. 'Get out of the kitchen before Lwalida catches you!'

'But we're hungry,' says Fatima. 'Give us bread, Amina, don't be so mean.'

I look out of the window. Lwalida and Zayna are lost in gossip. I hate Zayna, and I fear her. She has an evil eye that used to see me on my way to school and greet me as I walked back. I used to pray she would go blind, but now that I stopped going to school I barely have any time left to pray. I turn to Fatima. 'Keep a watch!' Yasmin, who is only two, claps her hands. 'Shush,' I tell her, then step on a stool and reach up to the cupboard door where Lwalida keeps leftover bread and couscous.

It's locked.

'Open it, Amina,' Fatima urges. 'Hurry!'

I jump off the stool, empty handed. 'She's locked it.'

Yasmin starts crying.

'Shush!' I say, but this makes her cry even more. I grab an uncooked *msemen* and shove it into her hand. 'Here!'

Fatima and Yasmin start fighting over the piece of dough. 'Hush, both of you, hush!' But it's like trying to tell a pair of wild cats not to scratch. I throw a nervous glance out of the window, see Lwalida surrounded by a group of fishermen. None of them is my father. Lwalida lets out a bloodcurdling scream. My sisters stop fighting. The three of us look on, as Zayna and one of the men try to hold Lwalida up, but she is too heavy: her body slips out of their grasp and hits the hard yellow earth with a hollow thud.

I'M A MOLLY DOLLY

I wake up and for one small uninterrupted moment I think I'm back home. I can even smell the river, hear a swallow patching up her nest, high up in the eaves, feel the soft valley air gently teasing the tip of my nose. I open my eyes. I'm in bed. My stark naked body is covered with a white cotton sheet and a thin green blanket. The wooden shutters on both windows give out a little squawk every now and again, whenever the breeze compels. Orange curtains rise and fall with the same breath. Like a little orchestra, playing just for me. I like it here. I hope I can stay here forever and a day.

A bird cries high up in the clear blue sky.

Without really wanting to, I rewind.

Orange, like yellow earth soaked with freshly spilt blood.

This is when the wall crumbles into dust and the memory returns. The tape at the back of my eyes rewinds at demonic speed, I'm back to knowing what happened to home, what happened to me, what happened to everyone, including Bella. Memories. I wish they didn't exist. Life would be much easier without them. Forgetting all the bad that's ever happened, now there's a superpower I would like to have. Although, if I think about it, it's the happy memories that hurt the most.

A door opens. One of the whores walks in, carrying a tray. See? I could've done that, carry trays around all day and shit, they didn't have to throw me to the dogs. It's the little black chick girl with crazy yellow hair, the one Miki joke-proposed to, and oh how we all laughed. Believe her name's something like Diamond. Or is it Rust.

'Hello, Miki's whore,' I mock her in my head, but then I notice she seems kind of petrified. We stare at each other, me lying in my comfy clean bed, and her, standing glued to a spot in the middle of the room, and it is her eyes that chicken out first.

'My name is Pearl.' Okay. I was close. 'I brought soup,' she says, genuinely sounding just like Prissy, the girl who lies about knowing how to birth babies so Miss Scarlett ends up quite rightly slapping her. 'You must eat in front of me. Get back your strength. Boss said.'

I watch as she takes a few steps towards the bed, then halts. Oh come on, girl. I'm hungry. There's nothing to fear but fear itself don't you know. Who said that. Someone really stupid. I move to sit up, Pearl jerks backwards, the soup spills over the tiles. This is when I realise she's not afraid of something she's left behind, she's afraid of something she's encountering right now. Like me, for example. Ha and ha.

'Sorry,' she cries. 'So sorry!'

Christ can she be any more annoying. I would very

much like to slap her, in my best *Gone with the Wind* accent, but I'm not sure what Boss would have to say about that. Could be that I'm in plenty enough trouble as it is, and besides, I'm not in a mood for gnarling through another piece of gristle right now. Or ever again. Oh Mema! You would've laughed, you really would. Or maybe you would've cried.

You never know how the emotional people will react to any given situation, they are notoriously unpredictable. Thank fuck I'm not like them. I put up my hands, palms open, towards her. The universal sign of surrender. *Hände hoch*, as the Nazis seem to like them the best. My dad was a huge fan of the Second World War movies, and I was a huge fan of my father. Put the two together, no wonder my command of German language is such absolute *Scheiße*. Pearl's accent is thickly dusted with French. I reckon she's an ex-Sahara girl, and judging by what I've seen thus far into my latest misery quest, we may well be in Spain. But then again, I might be wrong. I have been wrong before I'm proud to admit.

So I just sit there, with my hands up, and I wait. Soon enough, but could've been a tad sooner, Pearl finally dares place the tray on my night table. I grab the bowl, ignore the spoon, and start slurping. Pearl sits on the chair under the window and stares outside, her eyes heaven bound. First of all, who said she could sit. And second, I thought she was meant to be watching me eat.

I finish off by licking the sides of the bowl until it looks as good as new. I used to do this when I was a child, lick my plate clean then put it back into the cupboard because it no longer needed a wash. Until my sister spotted me and told my mother, and that was the end of that little energy saving exercise. As a joke, I show it to Pearl. Her eyes, normally dull and black like pieces of wet coal, light up like the burning bush of Mount Sinai. Is Mount Sinai even in the Sahara?

'Very good girl,' she says. 'Boss will be happy with you.'

Boss.

I wonder whatever that gorilla with mist for brains will do to me next.

'You must get ready, little one.' This, coming from a woman half my size. Alright – two thirds. 'So quit frowning and start getting dressed.'

Bossy old pebble. She isn't old, of course, I doubt many whores get to outlive their tight arses and perky boobs which everyone knows start wilting the minute you hit twenty. I reckon she can't be more than a couple of years older than me. And I'm really young. Too young for all this palaver for sure. Oh well. Shit happens. I've been stolen and I've been robbed, and I've been placed into scenarios that have nothing to do with me, never had and never will. But shit *does* happen. Whatever you do, you must not sweat it.

And when was the last time I listened to Iggy Pop. I can't even remember, and that will go into my black book of bad things done against my person, with a double underscore.

I want more soup.

'First you must wash,' says Pearl. 'You slept for the

last four days. You are smelly bum!' Pearl pinches her nostrils, banter I'm sure. Still, I want to smack her worse than ever. 'Come. I take you to bathroom.'

I get up, wobble around on my sea pins, then I guess the soup hits the spot and I start to command more authority over my limbs. I'm still naked, of course, but hell, when was the last time I paid any attention to the state of my body. Pearl hands me a crisp linen towel and motions me to follow her. I walk close behind, dragging the towel along the cool floor, down the long corridor and up the stairs, feeling like I'm a cartoon duckling following her mummy duck, until we reach the bathroom. Yes, it's a bathroom alright, but not as I know it: this one comes with a finely-tiled terrace and a sunken pool and a fuck-off view of acres upon acres of bronzed earth and cutting-edge palm tree green. And on the other side – the sea. As blue and milky as a newborn's eye, the sea enveloped the land like an effervescent shroud. The sea! Could be my way out of here. I could swim across this sea, through the water; reach my freedom.

'Now you bathe,' says Pearl. 'Later you stare.'

Pearl seems anxious again. I can sense her anxiety; it makes me feel a bittrigger-happy myself. Shame, that, because I could've really done with enjoying this bath – scented by lemon and orange oils – and in the times to come I often wished that I did.

'Come on, woman,' says Pearl. 'Wash!' She leans over to hand me soap and I use this opportunity to splash her sorry black ass all over. Her eyes flash with surprise, and something else. I don't know what, and I don't really care. But it did look a lot like a murderous intent to me. Who would've thought it. Fluffy-top Pearl, all meek and silly and highly slappable on the outside. Probably as hard as fuck on the inside, which is a combination I would admire, providing I could be bothered. 'What did you do it for, woman?' She glances towards the door behind us. 'You want to see me dead is that it?'

No, that wasn't it: I definitely didn't want is to see Pearl dead. I clamber out of the bath and offer her my towel. She bursts into laughter. 'You are one strange girl! Do you know? Strange.' She snatches the towel out of my hand and pats herself dry. It's hot out here, and her light yellow cotton dress will dry in no time, but I don't suppose any black girl worth her salt would appreciate getting her precious locks wet. She kisses her big white teeth all over, then throws the towel back. 'Your pussy is dripping. Dry it. Boss is waiting.'

Just when I thought I'd heard it all.

I feel weird, wearing the pale blue sundress Pearl made me squeeze into.

'Get in, skinny girl! And stop glaring, I am not falling for that crazy eye thing you do no more!'

It was a child's dress. How am I supposed to fit into a child's dress, and what sort of a moron – Pearl aside – would expect me to? Fucking Boss. Fucking men, they're nothing but trouble I swear.

Pearl zips me up, skin and all. 'A little make-up now. Come. Sit.' I hesitate. I fear make-up in general and I especially fear the possibility I may end up looking like a child whore wannabe. What's Boss gone and planned for me now, that stupid tall fat monkey-spider mountain. I hate it when people make plans for me. Why not just shoot me instead. 'Come now, girl! Stubborn, like a mule… Sit! Let me make you pretty.'

I almost want to crack up a smile here. Except I'm no longer capable of smiling. Probably suffering from muscle atrophy, but at least I won't be getting wrinkles any time soon. There's now a tune playing in my head, over and over again. It's 'My Way', Sid Vicious version of course, *and now, the end is near and so I face the final curtain* (idiotic giggle). I wish I had a pistol tucked inside my dress, wish I could take down the audience that awaits my so-called appearance, I reckon I'd be able to mow down the front of house, before they got me from the wings. As long as I get Miki, I don't care what happens next. I'd get him in the balls first, then I'd get him in the stomach and last but not–

'There you go, girl!' Pearl gets off her stool and takes a step back. I know I look like a painted troll, but she seems dead pleased with her handiwork nonetheless. 'Shame no mirror. Girls cut themselves with glass. And sometimes each other.' She cuts the air with her arm. 'Swish, swish. Not very nice.'

As I follow her back downstairs, I wipe off some of the make-up, and rub it into the back of my hand until it disappears. I would love to smudge it all over my face, end up looking like a black hole where red and green planets go to commit suicide, but like I said, for some strange reason I don't want to see Pearl dead.

We walk past my bedroom. I long to go back to that bed, back to the oblivion I emerged from far too soon. It's not as if I wish I was dead, more like I'd like to be cryogenically frozen until all the murdering assholes and also stupid people and people with good intentions – especially them – have been annihilated, so with a list as long as that I guess I'd be in for one hell of a snooze. Which would suit me just fine.

The moment we hit the outside, I can feel the hidden peepers crawling all over me. How do I do this, how do I always succeed in being the most interesting girl in the village, and without even trying. I must be a natural born people's person or something, as well as a guy magnet; probably all the good karma I accumulated in my previous lives. Although I'd much prefer to be a runt, blend in with my runty surroundings, live a runty life, die a runty death. Nothing wrong with that, is there now.

Pearl leads me to a small building positioned right on the edge of a cliff. View to die for, as some would surely declare. Oceans deep, valleys low, mountains high, most people seem to get off on that sort of thing. Not me, though: I'll take the woods any time, and a river with a sandy beach; a willow tree to fasten my little black boat to; a burning bulrush in my hand chasing the mosquitos away; oh how I wish I could have a go at being a part of my own little parcel for once, revel in the view of the palm of my hand, play hide and seek with Danube eels–

Ew. I hate fucking eels. Pearl must've spiked my soup, there's no other explanation for this sudden upsurge in my so-called will to live.

The building looks like a mini-version of one of those Hollywood mansions I saw on TV, with a solid concrete frame, gleaming white walls and miles of thick green glass. The view involves acres of flat greenness with random yellowing treetops poking up in twos and threes, nowhere to hide from the murderous sun. There's no tree older than seven or eight years amongst the lot. I can tell, because my dad liked to teach me stuff, especially about nature. Nature was his best thing ever. He used to take me and my sister for big adventure hikes into the forests that surrounded the three sides of our town, the fourth boundary being the river. Sometimes we'd walk, which I liked because my sister was a lazy girl who hated subjecting her fat little body to any unnecessary movement, and her huffing and puffing used to annoy my dad, and delight yours truly. Other times we'd drive and walk, and others still we'd bike off into the wilderness, and never look back. Alright, we did go back in the end, return home tired but victorious, and my sister ran straight for Mum's skirt. I guess I never liked to look back, not then and not now. So what am I doing, looking. No. Not for me the nostalgic preoccupation of a girlie kind, nor cutting my precious eyeball trying to see what's around the next corner.

I force-focus my attention on the stupid view. So here we have the said acres of grass-infested valley, tree-scattered slopes and a bold mountain to cherry the top. The sky is blue as King Solomon's ass, mottled with bursts of self-imploding clouds, rejoicing in their newly found freedom before the breeze eventually disperses it into oblivion. Poetic or what and can I throw up now.

'Hey! Girl! No time for daydreaming!' I lower my eyes to find Pearl's already firmly set on me. She looks a mix of tired, nervous and relieved. 'You go in now.' Suddenly I'm hit by a colossal wave of separation anxiety. I don't want to go in, and most certainly not without Pearl. I place my hand on top of her lower arm. She moves away, folds her arms tightly around her chest. 'Now, girl! Do not let him wait!'

I growl, but my heart is hardly in it. Still, it's enough to scare Pearl, who backs the fuck into the blistering sun. Human nature, eh. You grind a couple of hellhounds to rubble with your bare teeth and they judge you by it forever more.

BOSS

Where are you, Princess; where are you, girl? Eh? Playing tricks on me again? Fooling around with Daddy, are you, little Princess? Like a brush of fresh air, you are to me, my little friend. People, they scare far too easily. Doesn't take much. A raised eyebrow, and they are already shaking in their boots. I could be raising my eyebrow for a number of reasons. All harmless. Like for example, to remove a droplet of sweat from my forehead. Or to hold that thought. Or to appear a bit rascally, well why not? This is a very serious world we live in, and a little bit of jest should be welcomed, not feared.

Oh Princess! Oh my faithful slithery friend, come out come out wherever you are, it's time for a trick or treat, it's time to be nice to Daddy.

IT'S A BOY!

It's cool inside the building. The light-sensitive windowpanes allow for the shade to envelop, a rare quality when it comes to windows, not that I give a shit.

'Come… Come.' The voice seems to ooze out of the walls, thick and slimy just like its owner. 'Enter my humble abode, my favourite girl in the whole wide world, just follow the corridor and you'll find me.' I do as the walls tell me, and wind my way down into a large room occupied by one huge lilac armchair and not much else. This is probably the best space I've ever had the mixed pleasure of entering. All the walls are made out of glass, and although the fuck-off view is still lurking in the background, it has been made pleasingly visceral by the obscuring effect of the magic glass.

'Come here,' says the armchair. Like Alice in Wonderland, I walk over in awe and hope there will be cookies.

Boss greets me with an ear to ear grin. He's wearing only a mini skirt and a snake. Move over Alice, enter Mapplethorpe. The snake is a cobra, no doubt about that. And not just any cobra – this is naja

naja, or Indian cobra, the archetypal snake many a nightmare is made of, although I can't say I dream in snakes much. I watched naja naja on *Survival*, fighting mongoose and spitting at people and I think swallowing up an entire hyena or a lioness, my memory's gone blurry on the exact details. This one here must be a baby, as it is no more than a metre long, and as everyone knows adult cobras reach three to four metres in length on average. I wish I became a zoologist like my dad wanted me to, and maybe I still could one fine day if God decides to give me a break already.

'Sit here, next to me. No need to be shy. And don't worry about Princess, she's all spent.' Boss points at a leather cushion to his left. Having finished taking in her majesty the cobra, I can't help but noticing Boss's legs are sunk knee-deep in a metal bucket full of stuff that to my untrained eye looks a lot like wet cement. I manoeuvre my ass onto the edge of the cushion, as far away from his hairy white legs as I can without toppling over and waking up the snake. 'Vulnerability is the key,' says Boss. 'Every truly powerful man has a vulnerable side. It's a fact.' He leans towards me, half-squishing *ahem* Princess. 'The most powerful men amongst all men, they don't mind showing their vulnerability. Ay. They don't mind exposing their soft parts, not one little bit.' He flashes me a smile, pikey golden jewels here, there and everywhere. 'On the contrary: the most powerful men of all, they'll use their vulnerabilities to their advantage, like for example, to become even more powerful. Are you getting me, runt?'

I decide to reserve my judgment.

He laughs, then lifts Princess's floppy head to his lips, gives her what I hope to be a brotherly kiss. 'This one, she doesn't talk.' He's pointing at me, by the way. Not the snake. 'Doesn't fuck, either. Looks like a boy. Like a little vagabond. Ay ay – what are we to do with her?' He stares at me. 'You do have a tongue, right? Show me.' I offer the tip of my tongue. 'More,' he says. 'Show me more.' I pull it all out, quickly, and fold it back into my mouth before the cobra gets it. Boss screams with laughter. He sounds like a squealing November pig after the first knife pierced its throat: surprised, angry and euphoric from the last ever adrenaline rush to course through its bristly body. My dad could never kill a pig. He tried, and fainted every time. I offered to stand in, do what needed to be done and move on, but all the adults saw was this four-year-old girl trying to be cute, loving her daddy to death. They laughed and cooed and kind of looked down on my dad. So he got angry with me. Didn't say as much, but I knew by the way he walked beside me on the way to Saturday market, I knew he felt humiliated and it was all my fault for being so stupid that now he wouldn't even hold my hand, and it was all I could do to keep up the pace, weaving in and out of his path, trying to make it better by singing to him and making little butterfly jokes, but he wouldn't have it, he'd have none of it whatsoever.

'This one here, she ain't biting anyone for a while. Told you,' Boss shakes Princess at me. 'She spent, girl, she empty sack. See?' He then offers me the inside of his right arm. It has two red marks. At first I think *vampires*. Naturally. Next it dawns on me that these were snakebite wounds. Some of my cool impenetrable exterior must've cracked for a split second there, because Boss is quick to add, 'No need to fret. I asked Princess to do it. *Mea pulpa*.'

Boss chucks the snake on the pile of floor cushions. It just stays lying there, motionless and exhausted, like a floppy rubber toy. 'Touch the cement. Check if it's set.'

So it really is a bucket full of cement he's decided to dip his feet into. I crawl closer, knock on the semi-hardened surface. My knuckles leave small indents. Boss checks it out, yawns. 'Waiting's the worst part.' He sighs. 'I was going to ask you to read to me, but of course you're mute. Like a swan.' I glance at a pile of books on a small table next to him. They seem to be highly coordinated, according to the colour of their cover. There's a pile of green books, and red, and black. The black is the tallest pile. *The Rebel* by Albert Camus is on the top of the red pile. Sergei Yesenin's *Selected Poems* crown the green. His treatment of books, as well as the fact that a person like him should own any, should be doubly offensive to the book lover within, but frankly I'm too tired to entertain more drama. And besides, Boss is watching my every move. 'Ay, Sergei Yesenin!' He sits up, opens his arms and starts reciting:

Farewell, my friend, don't speak, don't shake my hand;
Please don't despair and don't frown your brow.
To perish in this life is nothing novel,
Although to live, of course, is also nothing new.

Boss wipes his eyes with a back of his hand. 'Pheasant boy, he was, just like I – and yet, what beautiful words, eh.'

Yeah – considering they came from a gamebird. I so envy Princess right now. Wish I could curl up next to her, and sleep forever.

Just then, a whore enters the room. It's the platinum bombshell Miki fed dirt to at the event of Bella's termination. She's not pleased to see me. Click-clack, her pointy golden stiletto heels punctuate her entrance.

She stops next to the armchair, squeezing her big backside right in the middle between me and Boss. He won't have it, though. 'Ay Nico, why you being so rude? Move over, babe, so I can see the runt.'

'So sorry, darling.' Nico does what she's told, but sneaks me an evil glare all the same. 'I want you to have eyes only for me, is that a sin?'

No it's a *pulpa*. Boss looks sore, rises both his eyebrows at me. 'I don't think my poor mother brought me to this world so I can discuss a philosophy of sin with a whore, what do you say, runt, what do you say, eh?' I hesitate to give him an answer, mostly on account of not speaking, but also because I find it highly suspicious whenever anyone comes across as double keen to learn what I have to say. 'Etiquette of sin is a grave and technical matter, one that states this thing and another, yet more often than not both at the same time, so to claim that one thing is wrong and the other is right would be the same as choosing to drink milk when what you really want to drink is orange Tango.' Pregnant pause.

'Except of course you also really really want to drink milk.'

Seriously.

Nico laughs. 'You're so funny, darling, like you went to Hollywood academy for actors and jokers!'

Boss flips the armrest cover. I see there's a button hidden under there. 'I didn't call you here to indulge in a small talk, eh! I called you to tell me what's the temperature like out there.' He checks underneath his skirt. 'And also to give me a blow job.' Nico drops to her knees. 'Not yet, you silly woman. First things first, and for the businessman like myself the first port of call is always – what?'

'Business?'

'That's right, my little goose.' Boss reaches into a leather briefcase to his right, takes out a fat wodge of American dollars, then peels off a couple of notes and stashes them into Nico's ample décolletage. 'My ears and my eyes, eh, here you go. Now talk to me about the weather.'

'First of all, Boss,' Nico purrs like a Persian cat's ass. 'The boys all seem very happy with their work and living conditions. Rob is back from the mountains, healed up nicely and keeping out of the coop, just like you instructed. Miki, on the other hand, is walking around like he's number one, screwing all your girls, bossing your men about, laying down the law, so basically nothing new there – Miki does what Miki wants.'

Boss bites on his lower lip. 'Is that so?'

Nico purrs up a notch. 'Yes. I would say Miki likes to give the impression he's running the show. But I tell everyone he ain't. He ain't the boss, I tell them, Boss is the boss.'

Boss winks at me. 'I couldn't put it more eloqueous myself!' He pats his lap. Nico drops onto it, making gurgling sex noises. 'So to recapitulate: Miki's out there, screwing my whores and telling my boys what's what, making it look like he's the boss, not me?' Nico nods. 'Right. And you're not saying this because you want to turn me against Miki, so I end up punishing him for what he did to you the other day, eh? Humiliated you in front of everyone like he did?'

Nico spits out Boss's finger she's been licking and sucking on like it was covered in the most delicious – for some reason I don't seem to be able to think of anything delicious right now. 'No, Boss, I'd never in a million–'

'I know you wouldn't, Nico,' says Boss. He's now stroking her long scraggy locks as if she was his pet Yeti. 'Because do you know what would happen to you if I ever caught you trying to manipulate a man like me, eh?' He turns her head towards me, forces her to look at me. I reckon this type of behaviour would've made me feel uncomfortable in the past. This violence. Trouble is, I can no longer remember what it felt like to be a person who abhors violence. I quite like it, these days, the violence. It grows on you, like ivy, and you grow on it, empowered by the venom, you grow down, way downtown, until you turn into a dweller of places low, dank and dark that exist just below the earth's surface, and you become a trap for all that choose to walk in the sun. If I was talented, and also not a prisoner of the crazy mother fucking pimp, I would definitely create a brand new comic book, called something like, *Erebus Rising*, or simply *Eleusinian Mysteries*, and I'd throw in a lot of different dark elements, make it a comic to end all comics. Except for *Dylan Dog*. I wouldn't want to cause demise of the greatest dawg of them all, I'm sure the underworld is big enough for both of us. 'I'd set the runt here to dig your lying cheating scheming whoring heart right out of your chest cavity with no other tool but her own teeth and nails, eh? I said, *eh*?'

'Yes, Boss,' Nico whispers.

'Sorry, what was that?'

'Yes, Boss!' Nico's voice pops out loud and clear this time around.

'That's better,' he says. 'Miki's a fool, that's why I like him. He's a fool who doesn't know he's a fool, who thinks other people are fools he can trick into doing as he pleases. But he is afraid of me, and isn't quite foolish enough to think I'm a fool, and if he does he has yet to show it. Until then, he will remain one of my most trusted employees.' Boss gives me a pair of googly eyes. 'After Jett. And this one here.'

Hey. What's just happened? Have I just been promoted to bodyguard a village idiot of brutal yet lofty persuasions? Can't say I feel especially chosen. And what the hell is wrong with my destiny. Other people's lives, they tend to unfold like a story of water: flowing mostly down the hill, sometimes above the earth, sometimes underneath, dropping below the surface when the going gets tough, spreading into ponds and puddles when it becomes easy again. My life, on the other hand, seems to follow a trajectory of an autumn leaf, as I continue to get tossed around by the winds that grow ever more wintery with each new gust. I live the story of air, but I dream the story of water.

I suspect Boss's eloqueousity may be rubbing off on me.

I listen on, but only because I have ears, as Nico proceeds to report on each and every one of the girls. She doesn't seem too enamoured by any of them, not even Pearl. You don't have to be Sigmund Freud to guess she must see them as a threat.

'So the temperature's satisfactory,' says Boss. 'Not too cold, not too hot. Ideal. And great news about Rob, eh?'

Nico shoots me a real nasty this time. Oh I get it. Must be the love story of this millennium. A Whore and a Thug. Can it possibly get any more romantic. I don't imagine it actually can. 'Well, he was very brave.' She sounds forlorn, but looks gleeful. What's up with that. 'This one here got him real bad, he only came out of the coma two days ago. He's due for his rhinoplasty later on this afternoon, thank heavens.'

'No need to thank them,' says Boss. 'But you can thank me instead.' He points towards his cock. Nico smacks her lips, and falls to her knees so gladly you'd think this event unfolding right here and now is what she's been looking forward to the entire year, like giving this particular blow job is her Christmas morning opening-the-presents hour come early. Bet this is what makes a good whore, this talent to make it look like sucking your cock is her bestest wildest dream come true.

I can't say I'm over the moon to have to witness yet another pointless copulation act of sorts, between two human beings (of sorts). Don't think I'll ever get used to it, I mean being exposed to people screwing each other in front of me. Given the choice, I'd rather not. Thank you but no thank you. Go fuck yourselves some place out of my sight, mind and life. But even though I don't have a choice, I'm going to pretend it's otherwise, so I turn my back on their performance. The view outside looks far less disturbing all of a sudden, I note.

There's a rustling noise behind me. Boss says, 'Watch the bucket.' And then, 'Stop. Stop, I said!' Silence. 'Runt?' I ignore him. What's he gonna do, talk me to death? 'Ay, ay, we offended the runt. Get off.'

More rustling, Nico blows out a loud breath of fury, Boss tells her to go do her thing, and what is she waiting for, a written invitation to leave, and soon everything grows silent.

'Runt?'

I don't want to answer to that name for the rest of my no doubt short and miserable life. I stay put. Like I said, what's he gonna do.

'Gill? Eh? Pletty little gill?' For a moment there he has me guessing. Then I realise: Boss is baby-talking at me. Fuck sakes. I know some parents do this to their children, but mine never have. Not even with my (stupid) sister. My mum was all, *ein-zwei-drei*, get on with it and grow up already. My dad, whose choice of a bedtime story was Shakespeare and

Tolstoy, was hardly a man who'd choose to keep anyone, including his own children, infantilised by proxy. And as for Mema, she didn't even need to talk for me to understand everything – and especially the fact that everything was fine. 'Tuln alound and look at me. Plittty please.'

I turn around, but only to stop this unbearable baby-talk. Boss looks tired, all of a sudden, probably on the downer. 'Good girl. Good little Princess.' He lifts his legs and pulls the bucket nearer the chair. 'Getting a little stiff, ay. This vulnerability muscle, it trophies all too quickly, you got to exercise it all the time.' He smiles. 'You were right; it was not righteous to have that whore suck me off like that in front of you. Don't get me wrong, there's no better tart than Nico-tart. She's a natural. Unlike Bella.' And just like that, I can taste the blood in my mouth – Boss's blood. But somehow, and please don't ask me how, I know the time isn't right. Guess he can join the queue. 'Bella was your friend, eh? I'm sorry for what you had to witness, but it had to be done. Bella was vulnerable, but in all the wrong places. She made *me* vulnerable in all the wrong places. She told punters about me. She complained to almost every man she did the business with. Told them rubbish about me, told them lies. Like for instance that I have a small cock. Not true, ay. Ask any girl you want, she'll tell you it was a very silly fib. Oh, and she told that I beat my girls with a rusty chain. I don't – I have men to do that sort of thing, so I don't have to.' He checks my reaction, adds, 'Rough them up a bit, ay, but only for their own good. Anyhoo, I asked Bella to take it all back, and she said she would. So I planted Rob. She thought he was just another punter, so she went and did her thing again – even though she had taken it back already, even though she had promised on her mother's grave she would not be telling stories about me for as long as she lives. Which turned out not to be very long. I hope now you can see why she had to go – she just had to, and that's all I have to say on that subject.'

I couldn't really tell you what was it I saw at that very moment, or why, but suddenly it was no longer a vision of everlasting doom. Okay, it wasn't the dream of salvation, either. But a small speck of hope did get in my eye, I'm sure of that.

'I'm tired, is the truth. I must sleep.' Boss points at his feet buried in the cement. 'I need someone to watch over my vulnerability. Ay. Ever since you saved me from that rabid dog, I knew you're the one. To watch over me, as the song would have it.' Okay dear God et cetera, if you do exist, please, please prevent this man from bursting into a song. Right now, I don't think I could take it. So of course Boss doesn't start singing (total proof that God exists, as well as the perfect illustration of where his priorities actually lie). Instead, he pulls a chisel from under his seat. 'Here, take this. Your first assignment, setting me free. Break it up, but be gentle. Ay. No cuts or bruises.' He gives me a probing look. 'But what about your name, eh? I give you an important role, so I must give you a proper name.' He cocks his head to the left, like he's thinking or something. Two extra-long minutes later, he claps his hands and proclaims, 'I know! I shall call you Igor.'

NICO

There comes a day when you realise you're going to leave him. There may be a reason – he looks at another woman in a way that makes it clear that he's still only a boy, not a man you hoped he was, or it could be the fact that his early arrival home from work, once a source of delight, suddenly fills you with rage. In truth, the reason no longer matters, not on this day. Because today is the day you realise you're going to leave this man, no matter what.

Hope is always there to begin with; here, there and everywhere, like a breadcrumb trail leading you to the promised new land. You feel excited, you think to yourself, I'm going to be happy, really happy with this man. You take time in seducing him, over and over again, until he becomes putty in your hands. I have been married three times, and each time I knew, this time it's for real. Donna Summer knew it too, that's why she sang about it. But then, one day, you realise that, sooner or later, you're going to leave this one, just like you left all the ones that came before him. Could take a week, or a month, or a couple of years. But from that day onwards, you're looking for the way out.

BETTER OFF DEAD

My job is easy. I follow Boss about all day, sleep in the room next to him during the night. I rest when he rests. I eat when he eats. I read when he reads. Upon my written request, he managed to procure 156 copies of *Dylan Dog*, every single one in mint condition, not only spotless but also catalogued. Granted, there was a small red splatter pattern across a couple of copies, guess someone made a mistake of refusing to hand over their precious comic book collection. But all in all, it was a scoop. Turns out Boss reads a lot. Harold Robbins and Sidney Sheldon, mostly.

One time, after getting himself as drunk as a skunk by downing three and a half bottles of limoncello, he pointed a gun at my head and ordered me to write down five books he would most benefit from reading. Lucky for me I actually knew five books. Lucky for me I have read more than a stupid would read in ten thousand lifetimes.

I wrote:
1. *The Sound and the Fury* by William Faulkner;
2. *The Ravishing of Lol Stein* by Marguerite Duras (Boss is not sure about this one, 'A woman

writer? You need a cock to be a writer. The bigger the cock, the better the writer. Ay. I'd make a huge writer, ha-ha. Okay, I'll read it – for you, little Igor. Just for you.');

3. *Fuck America* by Edgar Hilsenrath (Boss's favourite title, 'That's funny, ay, and yet so wise!');
4. *Jules et Jim* by Henri-Pierre Roché, and
5. *The Idiot* by Fyodor Dostoyevsky.

I couldn't resist this last one, despite the fact I hated anything Dostoyevsky had ever written. I did toy with an idea of slipping in that other dreadful volume of his, *Crime and Punishment*, but thought better of it. Why rock the boat that ain't even sinking. Just as well I didn't, because Boss took one look at the list, said, 'Why would I want to read a book about idiots? I'm surrounded by them already; I need a story that'll fish me out of this idiot-soup. Choose something nice, ay, choose something that will make me more saintly.'

So I crossed out *The Idiot*, and wrote *The Prophet* by Khalil Gibran.

Boss scratched his head. 'A dirty Arab, eh? And a prophet, too? Do you want to brainwash me, Igor, is that what you plan to do to me?'

So I crossed out *The Prophet*, and wrote *Lux the Poet* by Martin Millar.

Boss seemed to like this one. 'Nice choice, little one! A bit of poetry will do me a world of good.'

I was bursting to point out that just because a book has the word *poet* in the title, it doesn't mean it's a *book of poetry*. But I didn't, of course. First of all, I no longer spoke. And second of all, I didn't much fancy the idea of getting shot in the head, accidentally on purpose. The vision of hell having so unexpectedly vanished off my horizon, I kind of wanted to stay alive for long enough to see what gets to take its place. And I kind of started to believe that what's coming couldn't possibly get any worse than what went down before. Then again, if I had myself a great fuck-off neon sign with Famous Last Words flashing across it in giant ultra-fluorescent letters, I'd make sure I placed my previous statement right up there, just below the title, and just in case.

The gun did eventually return into its holster and Boss went to bed to sleep it off. Once he woke up, he apologised profusely, promised he'd never do such a thing again for as long as he lived. I remained suitably serious and distant, but secretly I was already counting how many new comic books I could get out of this latest guilt trip.

Apart from that little glitch, Boss and I live side by side like two peas in a pod. Except of course I'm only pretending I'm a pea, and not only because I hate peas on account on having almost choked on one when I was, like, a tiny baby (and then again at the age of four; then again at the lower school farm outing where I thought it would be fun to try and drink an entire cup of freshly-shelled peas; and then of course there was this memorable incident that involved yours truly, a straw and a bowl of Russian salad at my first ever no-grown-ups-allowed New Year's party... so no, don't talk to me about no peas, please).

I continue to walk a couple of feet to Boss's right,

like an extension of his stupid self, pretending I'm taking it all in like a proper bodyguard, but in reality just going about my own business of spotting the random patterns, and trying to work them out. Like for example a human voice, which belongs to the kaleidoscopic order, with its unique vibrational signature continuing to set and unset in bright jaggedy patterns long after their source had shut the hell up. Or a blade of grass, twisting and turning under the sky as if obeying an invisible choreographer from way up high. The sky itself also belongs to the order of troupes: I closely observe as it opens and closes its vast shutter to allow the passage of sun, moon and stars, all moving in the same rhythm as a single blade of grass, only in a different way. And, as I sit next to Boss during his so-called business meetings, I am conscious of the curvy fluid pattern of cardiovascular systems flowing through every man sitting around the table (the order of heart). Not a totally un-useful way to kill time, tracking the individual heart patterns of these pathetic men-creatures. 'You just never know what may prove useful and in what way,' Mema used to say, so it must be true.

The best thing of all, Boss had taken me off the meat market. With all the other more voluptuous – and more or less willing – girls in his stable, no wonder no one was exactly fighting over my sweet piece of ass, but the threat was always there. The threat of some ugly old guy – a devoted father of two, a loyal husband, faithful civil servant and a pillar of community – climbing on top of me and taking his money's worth, his pound of flesh whether I like it or not. This whole scenario seems to me way worse than a straight forward rape, which at least implies the element of randomness and eliminates any possibility of a woman's participation. Ask any whore. And if she tells you otherwise, then she's either too proud to tell the truth, or she's a man.

Talking of which, rape that is, I remember my mum having a conversation with her friend – a proof that my memory ought to serve me much better than it already does. I was only like five or six, so they were killing themselves trying to make their gossip as child-confusing as possible, not realising of course they were not dealing with a child, but me.

'Terrible news about that poor girl,' said Mum. 'In the papers this morning, you know?'

Rozi, her friend, went, 'The one who jumped off the balcony? I know! What a shame!'

'What else was she supposed to do,' said Mum. 'Give in?'

'She never stood a chance,' said Rozi. 'Three men, against one pretty little blonde.'

'I thought it was five.'

'Five? Well that makes even more sense. One little blond bird, against five beasts.'

'They would've torn her apart,' said Mum. 'You know?'

'I know,' nodded Rozi. 'But they didn't get to her in time.'

'Those animals!'

'Exactly. I read one of them tried to save her – and we know why, don't we! – but she managed to set herself free, and jump.'

'From the tenth-floor balcony,' said my mum. 'She knew she would be better off dead.'

'Bless.'

'Yes, bless her soul. Hope she finds her peace.'

I didn't like that story then, and I like it even less now. The way I see it, the girl was dead because she was too proud to get what was coming to her. I'm not saying she deserved to be raped or anything, what I'm saying is I'd rather fuck five men I don't particularly want to fuck, than choose to smash myself against a pavement, scare the little kids and dog walkers, make a general nuisance of myself, and, most importantly, totally destroy every chance of ever inflicting a suitable vengeance on those raping mother fuckers for helping themselves to my body without my permission, like I was a leg of roast lamb, theirs for the taking.

'Let's talk about something else,' said Rozi, pointing her eyes towards me. 'She's listening to every word we're saying.'

'She's only a child,' said my stupid mum. 'She wouldn't understand.'

I felt so disappointed with my own mother that I chucked the cheese pastry I was eating on the floor, and stormed off the veranda. As I grew older, it became clear to me that most adults are simply too dull to notice a bright spark, and all too inclined to stamp it out when they do accidentally happen to spot one.

'There are times when it is wise to hide your brightness,' Mema said once. 'Until one fine morning you wake up and discover it is safe to shine again.'

Well, Mema.

I'm still waiting.

Another best thing about becoming Boss's bodyguard is that no one gets to give me a dirty look any more. They wouldn't dare, not even Miki. I'm Boss's pet, but also his guardian demon – a wasps' nest no one dares to touch.

For now.

I'm well aware that my position here is precarious, to say the least, and by its very nature temporary. What goes up must come down, and the logic behind my own meteoric rise practically guarantees that one hell of a crash is to follow, which means I need to get myself a parachute.

So the next time Boss makes Princess dope him, I wait to check whether he's struck by euphoria or stupor. Who knew cobra's venom could be abused in such a user-friendly fashion. Guess *Survival* never covered all the different ways of getting high on animal's inbuilt defence mechanisms. When I see his head droop towards his chin, all floppy and deserted, I pull Princess out of harm's way and drape her around a branch of the dead tree Boss had planted into a pot filled with rocks specifically for this purpose. The first time I went to save her ass from being squished by the comatose Boss-mountain, the stupid snake panicked and gave me a dry bite. At the time I had no idea that snakes could opt out of releasing the venom into their prey, so the moment she sunk her needle-like fangs into my forearm, I hit the floor, and began to experience increasingly severe

– not to mention all too real – breathing difficulties. Next, my eyesight started to blur into the foggiest Turner, my heartbeat went into a drumming frenzy, and I honestly felt like I was about to meet my maker. But I didn't. Instead, I just laid there for a while, spreadeagled across the cool marble floor, before concluding I must be immune to snake venom, springing up to my feet and walking over to the fridge to make myself a refreshing salami sandwich.

That was the first and the last time Princess had a go at me. Nowadays, if for example I sit on her by mistake, all she needs to do is make this little hissing noise, and I'm off of her like a shot. Never knew it was so easy to reach an understanding with a snake. I must admit I'm starting to like Princess – a lot. She really is the coolest, almost as cool as this mad tomcat individual I once had. Well, never *had* him, of course. Only stupid people think they own other creatures, like animals, and each other. But I don't want to discuss stupid people right now, too boring for words and also the subject most likely to make me angry. I'd rather continue talking about snakes, and the fact that they have this thing called Jacobson's organ, which is an auxiliary olfactory sense organ that regresses at some point during human foetal development, which allows them to communicate with one another by using pheromones, not words. This is almost an exclamation mark worth of cool, except of course only stupid people use exclamation marks in order to inform other stupid people that this is the point where you gasp. Fuck's sake (exasperation mark), what's with me and the stupids today, and oh how I wish I was immune to them, as well as the snake venom.

With Princess hanging in her beloved grey branches that I like to think remind her of home, and Boss softly snoring in his armchair, I am free to go off and explore. It's an early evening, and everyone's buzzing around in search of after-dinner mints. The whores work in shifts, day shift runs from 8am to 6pm, and night from 10pm to 8am. It's just before 8pm, and they are all here, sitting around the outside table, doing each other's hair and nails, boogying about to the pop beat rattling out of a battered ghetto blaster, and generally frolicking around the place like a regular gaggle of young, care-free girls. And if I must choose, I'd still rather have me a bunch of whores – the very thought of a group of young, care-free girls makes me feel suicidal, not to mention homicidal. Or is it the other way around.

The whores pretend not to notice me, but of course they do. I can tell by the way their movements slow down, their manner becomes more measured and affected. Their bodies heave up and away from me in a blink and you'll miss it kind of way, except for the little known fact that I almost never blink. Reckon this type of behaviour is what you'd call *shunning*, designed to potentially hurt the shunned person's feelings. It doesn't bother me, though. I know they think I'm crazy, and also a sell-out, despite the fact I never fully made it into their precious whore order. Even when I was sharing a cage with a couple of them, at the back of the lorry that had brought us here, they treated me like I was some kind of a wall fly they would've liked to squish but didn't want to risk getting their hands dirty, or their nails broken. To give them some credit, right, most of them seemed rather preoccupied with an unmistakable lack of plush work surroundings they were promised upon the start of their long journey away from home. Whatever the enlisting guy told them, over a cocktail and maybe a slap-up dinner at the best barbecue joint a couple of villages away from the one they hailed from, I bet he neglected to mention anything about spending days on end locked up in the back of a stuffy lorry, and taking turns in appeasing the local Checkpoint Charlies in the nearby bushes, as a way of making a payment towards the free passage. True, the cages were only introduced after one girl managed to break free by jumping out of a fast moving truck. We had to wait for ages until the search party returned, pissed off and empty handed, closely followed by an arrival of a lorry that delivered the cages. How much more medieval can you possible get, was what I thought, but what I did was jump in before anyone even had to ask. I sat in next to Bella. She looked scared, and she smelled funny, like she might have just peed herself. But she still gave me a little smile I almost wished I could return.

I push my way through the body-block, the whores make a few obligatory aggrieved noises that by design will never change the world. I sit on the table, right in the middle of their supper leftovers and make-up paraphernalia. Not one of them dares stare at me directly, all I can feel is a prickle of a few side-sweepers. Nico comes at me from nowhere, trust her to take a stand for everyone.

'Can I help you, Igor?'

She's inspecting me in the same way she'd inspect an impotent but moneyed punter: the sooner she finds the right way to help him out, the sooner he'll be out of her life. Yes, Nico has seen it all before, and lived to tell the tale. She can handle a brat like me with her eyes closed and her hands tied behind her stupendously curvaceous backside. People like her, who have insisted on surviving times and events that really ought to have killed them, they tend to be patient. For they will have their time in the sun yet, when everyone will finally see what all the sacrifice was really about.

Blah. Blah. Blah.

'Are you lost?' she asks. 'Hungry? Would you like something to eat? Pearl could make you some fried chicken, eh?'

Pearl leaps off her chair, sends it off flying into a couple of girls huddled at the back.

'Ouch!' One of the girls holds onto her toes. 'Watch it, puta!'

Pearl springs a resounding slap around the girl's face, Nico catches her hand before she's able to have another go. 'Oi, oi, oi! Pearl! That's enough. Enough, I said.' She shoots a glance over to the group of men, sitting on a bench underneath a fig tree, smoking tobacco. They seem oblivious to the drama unfolding in the chicken coop. Must've seen it all before, anyway, girls cutting into one another like rabid cats, yet complaining like right little bitches when a man

52

roughs them up as part of his noble mission to spread the love. 'Go to the kitchen, now!' Pearl takes an unsteady step in the direction of the house, then stops and turns around. She's staring me down hard. Yes, I think I do fancy me a bit of fried chicken, after all. 'I said *now*, Pearl. Go girl, go!'

Pearl staggers away.

'You have to excuse Pearl,' says Nico. 'She's had some bad news from home.'

From home. Well how about that. Pearl has a home – no doubt in some godforsaken village inhabited with incestuous tribe of possum eaters. But still. A home is a home. And what does she do? She abandons it in favour of making her living by fucking any monkey with a handful of dollars and a reasonable hard-on. Worse than monkeys, actually, these men. Shifty looking businessmen with Lego sports cars; local government officials, balding and wilting in every direction, desperate to prove they still have it by fucking a whore; peasants, their sense of shame only equalled by the immense hunger at the pit of their stomachs, the same unsatisfiable hunger that lined the bellies of their ancestors ever since that freaky turn of cosmic ordering created their bloodline in the first place. Plus, she is always on call to pleasure the soldiers of fortune Boss employed to look after his interest. This means she is never really off duty, because if a soldier comes a-knocking, Pearl must drop everything and go down to the fuck-hole with him.

Fuck-hole is my term of endearment to describe the little white house, located a few hundred metres down the hill from the main buildings, used exclusively for the purpose of entertaining the troops. It's currently under a lock and key, because a few of the boys decided to have a Sharing Party, the time-honoured tradition of sharing a female body in a competitive fashion with a purpose of establishing which man can do her the most sexual favours, whether she likes it or not. But then it all went terribly wrong.

What happened was this: just after midnight that night – Boss and I were still awake, watching a pirate copy of *Pulp Fiction* – a call came through to his brand new Nokia 2110.

'Who the fuck?' Boss yelled into the receiver. 'Blake? This better be good, I was just about to watch Bruce Willis getting buggered! Talk slower! Talk louder! Stop shouting!' After he hangs up, Boss got up and motioned me to follow. 'Those savages, they ruined another one. Now I will have to put an end to it, and then what are they going to do for fun around here, eh?'

We walked down to the fuck-hole. Well – he walked, I skipped and bounced, high on a cinema size portion of churros, washed down with two mugs of thick hot chocolate. 'Look at you,' said Boss. 'Like a frisky brown squirrel. Stop it, you're making me all dizzy!'

But I knew he was only saying it, and so I continued my slalom down the hill, hitting the door way ahead of Boss. The room was full of men, some half dressed and bloodied, and others pulled in from their night guard duties to help clean up the mess, except they did no such thing but instead just stood there and gawped at the scene of the crime, chain-smoking and sharing silver flasks of firewater. Nico was also there, holding a body of a girl. I couldn't quite make out who she was, until I recognised the pretty bracelet around her left ankle. I had spotted it straight off, the very first time I saw her coming out of a truck, only a couple of days ago. 'Fresh meat,' said Miki, who never failed to get the prize for stating the obvious. The girl with a bracelet looked all sweet, sleepy and small. Smaller than even Pearl. I mean, *really* small. Like a small child small. The bracelet around her ankle suited her well, a delicate golden thread with a spatter of single red roses that winked as she walked. I remember thinking this should not be allowed, or something on those lines, but shrugging it off as yet another potential burden in making. And I prefer to travel light.

The girl wasn't dead. She made gurgling noises, like a fountain that was running out of water. Someone had covered her up with a blanket, but the pool of blood had spread from underneath and across the floor all the way up to the door.

Boss came in, it took him a moment to suss out the situation.

'Jett!' He barked. 'Is Jett here?'

Miki pushed through. 'Here, Boss!'

'Are you Jett?' asked Boss.

'No, Boss, I don't believe I am.'

'In that case, fuck off!'

Jett appeared. 'Boss?'

'Take her to the mountains,' Boss said. 'Leave her at the edge of the forest. The Hill People will take care of her. Or something will. And whatever you do, do not enter the forest, eh? Do not cross the line.'

'Yes, Boss!' I watched Jett as he lifted the girl off the floor, as gently as you would a wounded butterfly, then carried her out of the room. I felt jealous, because I sort of fell in love with Jett ever since he had stood up for me when everyone else, including Boss, seemed all too keen to feed me to the Hellhounds. And yeah, I know it's not exactly right to feel jealous when a man you hardly even know is trying to save a half-dead girl, but hey: welcome to my world. At the end of the day, she chose to be here. I didn't. She chose to forsake her cosy little home for this magical kingdom where fuck-holes come true, and, I repeat, *I didn't*. Perhaps she really would've been better off dead, for everyone's sake.

Well then: what was so bad about Pearl's news. I decide to quit hanging around this red and black hole where daemons come to roost, and do a bit of snooping instead.

HIPS LIKE CINDERELLA

Mema told me she was in love once.

'I was in love, once,' she said. 'Hey, bookworm! I'm telling you an important secret, so pay attention!'

I looked up from my book. 'I know, Mema.'

'What do you know, child?'

'I know you were in love,' I said. 'With Big Daddy. Until death did you apart.' I think. 'Can you be in love with dead people, Mema?'

She laughed. 'Of course you can! In fact, some folk believe that dead people make the best lovers.'

'Like Count Dracula?'

'Yes, a bit like that.' Mema pauses. 'But I wasn't talking about your grandfather.'

I put down my book. 'But you married him.'

Mema gave me a strange look. 'So?'

'So you had children and a house and cats and parties together.' I felt the fear creeping up from the pit of my stomach and spreading into my chest. Has Mema gone mad? I had heard that old people sometimes liked to go off with the fairies, never to return. Has this happened to my Mema? 'And you lived happily ever after with Big Daddy, no one else, the end.'

'I blame your mother,' said Mema. 'And that drivel she reads when she thinks no one's looking.' I didn't know what she was talking about. My mum never read anything. Dad did, all the time, just like Big Daddy used to when he was still alive. But Mum – never. 'Brainwashes good women into romantic scavengers!'

I didn't know what to say, so I said exactly what was on my mind. 'I think you have lost your marbles, Mema, I think you no longer know what you're saying.'

'Oh really?' Mema set her hands on her hips, like she always did when she meant business. 'What's your favourite fairy tale, child?'

'Cinderella.'

Mema rolled her eyes so high I feared they may never return to their sockets. 'And, dare I ask, what do you like about it?'

'Well first of all I like it when her mother dies, which is a bit sad, but at least Cinderella can now live happily alone with her father. After a while it turns out he never really loved Cinderella because he gets another wife, and totally betrays Cinderella by bringing this stupid woman and her two ugly daughters into the house, and he doesn't really care when they make Cinderella sleep in the ashes and eat potato peels.'

'Potato peels?'

'A-ha, that's what they give her for breakfast, lunch and dinner.' I take a sip of the cherry cordial Mema made at the end of every summer, and continue, 'So poor Cinderella, all alone and treated like a servant, she's still real nice to everyone and sweet and everything, but no matter how lovely she is, the stepmother and those two – may I say a swear word please, Mema?' She nodded. '*Bitches*, they are still treating her like – may I say another swear word please, Mema?' She shakes her head. 'Oooh Mema, it wasn't even going to be that bad! Anyway, they are treating Cinderella like *poo*, okay, and getting away with it, until Prince has a ball and invites all the girls in the Kingdom, and that means Cinderella too, but those horrid women still lock her away. Because they're really jealous of how great she is and also they're afraid of her. But she gets to go anyway, because she has these amazing friends, animals and birds, and best of all, she has a fairy godmother – I imagine she's a bit like you, Mema – on her side, so she goes to the ball and Prince falls in love with her at first sight and they dance all night – well, until midnight, and then the magic stops, and I really hate it when the magic stops like that but it's alright, guess it makes the story all the more exciting. So in the end, Prince does find Cinderella and they do live happily ever after and the stepmother and ugly stepsisters get the punishment they deserve. The End!'

Mema watched as I downed the rest of my drink. 'Some story. But tell me, if you could change anything about it, anything at all, what would that be?'

I didn't even have to think. 'I would shoot the stepmother and ugly stepsisters the minute they set foot into my house, then I'd pack my stuff and leave my cheating Dad to it, and then I'd go to the ball and get married to Prince all the same.'

Mema laughed. 'Glad to see your mother didn't manage to spoil all of you!'

The camp had two main buildings, plus the fuck-hole. One was Boss's fake Hollywood mansion; the other is an old-style hacienda, wrapped around a courtyard with a heptagonal fountain in the centre. If it wasn't for the total lack of happy reason for my being here, I would've probably loved this place. Still, I allowed myself to feel a certain amount of strictly platonic fascination with it, especially the veranda, with its arches covered in white and crimson-coloured, white-throated Morning Glory; fragrant, pinky-purple blossom Egyptian bean, and red and orange, tooth-like Firecracker vine. I used to read my dad's botanical encyclopedias, that's how I know who's who in the world of flowers. And yeah okay: I may have been a weird little girl, but hey – look at me now.

The left side and the middle of the building provided bedrooms for the whores and their keepers respectively, and the right housed the kitchen and the large dining stroke game room.

'I bought the limited edition Bonzini football table – only the best for my boys,' Boss once told me. 'I treat them well, they eat out of my hand, everyone's happy. You must give me a game of pinball one of these days, little Igor, and I'll show you the wizard at work.'

Tempting as this sounded, I declined his offer, despite the idle curiosity brought on by the maddening sense of boredom. There was so little for me to do around here, except follow Boss about his great Kingdom of Pussy Galore (working title), I was seriously considering stealing a gun and shooting somebody, perhaps even myself, just for a bit of fun. Saying that, I did attempt to sneak in once, it was a late dog-day afternoon, when everyone was down the pool, and Boss was sleeping it off back at the house. I was going to snoop through ladies' drawers and mess up their dressing tables a bit, maybe steal some stupid stuff from the men, like their precious hair gel and one sock out of a pair, but no sooner did I place my foot on the veranda than the smell hit me so hard it made me retreat like a bat out of hell, but obviously in reverse. The stink was like no other shit I have ever smelt before; in fact, it was not anything as plain bad as, say, toilets or unwashed bodies or rotten eggs. This particular stink was light and animated, almost aromatic at first, made out of high notes and silver threads that drew you right in, before turning into a tight noose that pulled you down into another world entirely, the world of rot and sheer wickedness, the world of boys and girls so lost they have long forgotten how to beg for mercy, or how to offer it.

'What is it, Igor?' Boss would ask, as we walked on by. 'Eh? What are you wrinkling your nose at? What can you smell?' He'd then take my hand, bring me in closer, check around for any spies, as well as spy lookalikes, then say, 'Is it death? Can you smell death, fast approaching our shores, cruel and unforgiving?'

As it turned out, Boss proved to be quite a superstitious character, prone to a spot of supernatural paranoia, especially when hitting a downer. Another thoroughly unpleasant thing he was prone to was spontaneous raptures. I had the mixed pleasure of witnessing this on my very first day, when he suddenly grabbed my foot, causing me to fall back on a pile of cushions.

'My God, Igor, you have a proper Greek toe!' He gently teased my second toe out of its terrified little curl. 'Look! It's almost a whole nail longer than your big toe, which means you have the power of extravagant perception, you know: the sixth sense!' He went on to explain how the second toe represented something he called an *inner vision*, or what I'd probably call an intuition if I was dumb enough to believe in any of that crap. According to Boss, most people in Ancient Greece had these giant second toes, on account of being super developed in both the spirit and I guess the body. '*Mens sana in corporate sano*! It's all about spiritual development, right, which is something most CEOs don't get, but I do, I know how to run the business with my soul, not my head.' He then kissed my forehead, whispered, 'I knew there was something very special about you the minute I saw you. And don't you be looking at me like that, throwing you to those dogs was only a test, and you passed it with flying colours, eh, just like I prayed and hoped you would!' He kissed my forehead again. 'My own little psychic weapon of choice, who would've thought!'

Boss's weakness for all things spooky quickly became my favourite thing about him, because although he often knocked himself senseless on Princess and other, more vigorous, prescriptions, I wasn't sure how I could use this to my advantage. But his taste for paranormal, well that seemed open for all manner of manipulation. Consequently, I never answered yay or nay about the nose wrinkle situation, keeping the man guessing became the name of the game.

I find Pearl sat at the kitchen table, head buried in her hands, not moving, not making a sound. I stand in the doorway and stare at her for a while. I could do anything to Pearl right now, kill her even. And she'd be none the wiser, she'd just drift away into oblivion without ever realising it was me who caused her demise. No story, no pain, nothing. And even though I have no intention of murdering Pearl, I feel annoyed at the fact that she will never know how I spared her life for no other reason but my compassion for another human being and the big warm heart pulsating in my chest.

But I want to do something. Look at her. So annoying. So pathetic. Oh I know, I'll make her cook me up a feast, fry me a couple of eggs with ham, and pancakes, and make me a chocolate birthday cake. Even though it isn't my birthday. I'll make her work for her living, there's nothing worse than an idle whore.

'How about some orange juice?' The voice comes from behind the door, scares the shit out of me. I pull back into the shadows, my heart beating so loud and clear I fear everyone must wonder what the fuck's up with the African drumming practice. I hear the steps, then a chair, scraping along the floor. Deep breath, and I'm ready to peep back in. I see Jett, sat down next to Pearl with his back turned to me, stroking her hair. My heart shrivels up into a painful twinge. 'You must have something, Amina. Come on, a little something, do it for me if not for yourself.'

Amina? What sort of a fucked-up name's that. And Jett, what the fuck. Doesn't he know that only the stupid people are nice to stupid people?

'You are too good to me, Jett.'

Too right.

Jett removes a stray lock off Pearl's, or whatever her name is, face. 'Drink up. You'll feel better, you'll see. You had a shock, there's no need to be brave.'

I wonder what he's talking about. But even more, I wonder how did I end up falling for an unavailable man. I'm no better than a stray dog, no self-respect whatsoever. And should I really be blaming Pearl for this. Bloody right I should.

Right on cue, she burst into tears. 'Sorry, sorry, I am so sorry…'

'No need to apologise,' says Jett. 'Better out than in.'

'What am I going to do?' Pearl looks up at him like he was her very own personal Jesus. 'I cannot stay here, not like this.'

'Just for a little longer, I promise,' says Jett. 'Act naturally, keep your cool, so no one starts suspecting anything, okay?'

My ears prick up. What have we got here? A prelude to mutiny? I'm so going to tell Boss on them.

Pearl blows her nose, nods. 'Okay.'

'Good girl.' Jett lights up a long brown cigarette,

inhales deep. 'Sorry – does this bother you?'

Pearl shakes her head. 'No. I am only sick in the morning, before breakfast.'

'How long gone are you now?'

'I am not sure. Two months, maybe.'

Well fuck me if I don't yelp out loud at this point. I really need to find out what's with all the yelping, before it spells the end of me. I'm about to leg it, but Jett's hands are already upon me. He drags me into the room and kicks the door shut. Pearl is standing in the middle of the kitchen, one hand over her mouth, the other clutching onto a table.

'I am doomed,' she keeps saying. 'I am doomed.'

'Quiet! Amina!' says Jett. 'Pearl! Be quiet!'

Pearl falls silent. I break loose from Jett's lovely arms, not because I want to, but because I don't. He's looking at me, all serious and grave and manly, but I swear there is a little twinkle in his eye. Did I mention I find Jett lovely? Maybe I'll end up writing a poem about him. Maybe I'll title it *Lovely Jett*. I make a sudden move to the left, Jett falls for it. I swap directions speed of lightning style, and make towards the other door. I grab the handle, but the fucker won't turn. How embarrassing. Plus, I now get to be killed by a man I thought I'd one day progress to marry, although the fact that he's had impregnated a silly black ass whore may cast a shadow over the happy event.

'Igor? There's nothing to be frightened of, okay?' Jett starts walking towards me, with his hands up in the air, palms facing out. Oh no, it's the *hände hoch* move, the universal sign of an imminent threat. My breathing is so shallow I feel like I'm about to grow a pair of gills. Jett stops a foot or so in front of me. He smells of man sweat. If this is what death smells like, then I don't mind dying. 'Don't cry, Igor.' He wipes the tears off my face. 'No need for tears. We can sort this out, the three of us.' He lifts my chin, may as well look at him. He's smiling. I'm not crying. 'We can sort this out.'

Phew. Turns out Jett wasn't having an affair with Pearl, and therefore he couldn't possibly be the father of her unborn baby. Apparently, she got pinned down by a punter who refused to wear a condom. He gave her a wad of money afterwards, and apologised profusely, asked if they could do it again some time. This news pleases me no end, but I hide it well.

'I do not trust Igor,' says Pearl. 'She crazy, and she Boss's girl, she tell him everything, and he will make me kill my baby.'

Correction: it is not a baby. It's only an embryo, a cluster of random cells that you could call a mushroom and still get away with it.

"I don't think Igor is Boss's girl.' Jett pulls a small notebook out of his pocket, pushes it over to me. 'And here's a pen. In case you'd like to write down your real name. Or anything else.'

I grab the pen, scribble down a word, push the notebook back. He reads it, laughs. Pearl looks in, which is a bit rude, seeing that the note was meant for Jett's eyes only, but what the hell can you expect from a common garden variety whore. '*Cop*? She knows you are a policeman! Well now we are all doomed, and it is all my fault!'

'Not your fault,' says Jett, 'And no one's doomed.' He offers me one of his lovely cigarettes, just like a proper good cop would. It's highly perfumed and I could smoke it all day long. 'Tell me, Igor, are you really Boss's girl?'

I shake my head. Pearl collapses on the chair, with relief I think. But seriously – what did she expect me to say?

'That's what I thought.' Jett checks his watch. 'I must get back, but first I need to know if I can rely on you.'

I nod.

'To look out for Amina, yes?'

I frown. Why the fuck would I want to do anything of the sort?

'I mean, *Pearl*, I need you to treat her like she's the most important person you've ever met.' Seeing the expression on my face, he adds, 'Pearl is the first person who has agreed to stand as a witness against such an important trafficker in more than a decade. And once Boss goes down, we're hoping that more women will dare speak out, which will put an end to other trafficking operations.'

'*Insha'Allah*,' says Pearl.

'*Insha'Allah*,' says Jett. 'Another thing; if anyone finds out Pearl's pregnant, Boss will make her have an abortion. They will not care about how it's done, either. And there's been enough blood spilled around here already.'

Jett looks sad. I get it. He's been sent to do his big job, all hush-hush and undercover, so he had no choice but to watch them kill Bella, and massacre that little girl with a rose bracelet around her left ankle, and who knows what else. I think he should be sad, I think he should suffer, but also I think he needs a hug. Not that I'm likely to give him one, that wouldn't be very cool, but if he married me, of course, the two of us could go and live some place far away from here, and hold each other in our arms whenever the demons come in the middle of the night. And also fuck a lot.

'So, Igor,' he says. 'Will you do it? Will you look after Pearl for me, until I organise her exit? And maybe yours, too?'

What Jett doesn't get is that this here *is* my exit. As in, I have exited. No more exits for me. I may go around pretending to plot how to use Boss's weaknesses to my advantage, but that's all it is – a little trick I play on myself, mainly because I no longer know what my advantage is supposed to look like. Another thing is, I'm tired. Princess and I reckon our wilderness days are well and truly behind us. So fuck you, lovely Jett, for coming out of nowhere, confusing my attempt to go with the flow, to live the life of water. I grab the notebook, write down what comes naturally.

They take turns in reading it.

'What is this?' asks Pearl.

Jett smiles. 'Let's just assume it's a yes.'

> *I was a child and she was a child*
> *In this kingdom by the sea*
> *I hate and loathe and I despise*
> *everything about Amina Lee*

R.E.S.P.E.C.T.

Days drag on by. All three of them. It's only been
three days since I promised Jett I would look out for
Pearl – aka Amina, whilst he calculates her escape
route, but it feels like ages. I wish to point out that the
idea of me looking out for anyone, especially a
pregnant whore in a middle of a *whore-konclager* is so
ridiculous it borders on surreal. Accordingly, if we do
end up getting caught, which we will, we could
always pretend we did it for art. Or we could say we
were only playing *Schindler's List*. I watched the
pirate copy with Boss only the other night. He began
crying from the moment the opening credits started
to roll, and continued throughout the movie, even
had to change his shirt mid-view because it was
soaked with his giant crocodile teardrops.

'Fucking Nazis! Fucking *Schutzstaffel*! See? See
what they did to us? Ouch. My nose is sore from all
the snot, ay.' He stuffed pieces of paper napkin into
each of his nostrils. 'Do I look ridiculous? Don't look
at me. I said, don't look at me, little Igor!'

I was very glad when the film was over, enough
melodrama for one evening, I thought. But Boss
seemed restless; disappointed, even. 'We have got to

watch it again,' he said in the end. 'With our eyes dry, this time. No more crying, eh, no more sediment. You Igor are very lucky you have no sediment to speak of. It's a blessing.'

The space oddity's right, I am lucky. I am blessed. What's there not to like; I don't speak. I don't feel. I try my best not to dream. I don't cry (despite what Jett says). I do get hungry, occasionally, which is how I know I'm alive. And, as living goes, I reckon my life is one of the more accomplished ones. It has a certain Zen quality to it, even if I say so myself.

We watched *Schindler's List* three times that night. At the end of the third viewing, Boss finally switched the TV off and said, 'There is no doubt left in my mind or heart; Ralph Fiennes must be punished for inciting crimes against humanity.' He then made a couple of long-distance phone calls, by which time I was already drifting in and out of my own movie, where Ralph Fiennes let me try on his boots, and the two of us plotted to run away together, far, far away where no one knew our stories. He offered me his hand, but when I turned to take it, I saw it was Jett I was really running away with.

My point? The game of *Schindler's List* idea is out. I don't think Boss would be take too kindly to any scenario which compared him to the core of Nazi terror apparatus he hated so much that even watching a movie on the subject proved enough to push the already thin line between fiction and reality to the point of psychosis.

I mustn't get found out, and because I made Jett a

promise, Pearl mustn't get found out either. I just wish Jett would hurry up and give me some indication of when, where and how. As things stand, I can only describe Jett's behaviour as avoiding strike ignoring. Like for example, he no longer sneaks a half-smile when I stand behind Boss during the regular daily drill, drawing dusty eights with the tip of my bare foot. Also, the moment he spotted me trying to catch up with him yesterday, he made a beeline for a couple of whores, then sort of pretended to lose himself in the most pedestrian of chats, until I got bored waiting and wandered off after a chicken. Ten minutes later, I saw him again, all the way down at the bottom of the molehill Boss had built his empire of smut on, catching up on his chores doubly quick, like he was making up for the lost time. I even waved at him a few times, discreet as can be, but he looked straight through me, like I was made out of glass. Personally, I think he's taking this escape thing a little too seriously, but what do I know, I'm no secret agent 005. Or is it 6. Never liked James Bond movies, and neither did my dad.

Must say, though, it's just as well I don't feel much, otherwise I'd probably start feeling a little bit rejected and forlorn right about now.

Despite tittering on the brink of inner turmoil, when Boss ordered me to tidy my ass so I could join him for a spot of Big City shopping, my heart skipped a beat. Jett was the only driver designated to driving the Merc. I'd love to see him try and ignore me with Boss watching our every move.

'The man has a certain *je ne sais quay*,' Boss once

said about Jett. 'The rest of them, nothing but a bunch of punks. Good for brandishing knuckledusters, and not much more. I have a certain reputation to uphold, ay, I'm a top notch international businessman. Can't be seen intergiggling with rednecks and such.'

The ride to Big City is pleasant enough, even though Boss seems stuck on Dusty Springfield and her stupid songs about love that in my humble opinion deserve a punishment far greater and more urgent than Ralph Fiennes. Sitting behind the wheel, Jett's as deadpan as can be, not to mention handsome. Wonder if he's FBI or CIA, and also if they are one and the same. I just hope he doesn't belong to Scotland Yard, or something equally archaic not to mention uncool. Bond, James Bond. Hope he's not that one.

We stop at the very front of a department store, with an eager beaver valet kissing our ass all the way into the foyer, and another taking care of Boss's precious Mercedes Benz. I notice Jett checking his inside pocket, for his gun, what else. A driver, a bodyguard, an FBI agent. Truly a man of many talents, as well as the man I really, really want to kiss like I've never wanted to kiss anyone ever before in my life, not that I can remember.

This realisation isn't a particularly happy one. *On contraire mon cher*, to paraphrase our friendly erudite not to mention polyglot Boss, it only serves to dim my mood somewhat. Because, long before my life made the so-called shocking and traumatic turn that got me to where I stand now, I had woken up one morning and I just knew that there was not one single feeling left that I actually believed in. To go back on such undisputable knowledge would be like eating your own vomit. I knew a person who did exactly that, by the way. Her name was Sofija. Didn't actually know her, as such, but used to see her rummage around my old town, so drunk and disorderly even the police kept their distance. She did this trick where she would lift her skirt, and show her pussy to anyone unlucky enough to be looking in her direction. Bet she did it for a good reason, though. Bet it served as a deterrent for a kind of man who liked nothing better than to copulate with an unconscious female, believe the correct term is necrophilia. The story went that Sofija lost her husband, children as well as her marbles in a traffic accident, then promptly took to drink. A friend of mine, well not really a friend, just somebody I used to walk to school with whenever I forgot to avoid him, once told me he saw Sofija throwing up all over the pavement, then hoovering the whole thing back in again.

'She did it for the alcohol content that was still available in her sick,' he explained, like a good doctor's son that he was. 'She was that desperate for drink.'

So there you go, fall in love with that.

'Please stop.'

I'm standing very close to Jett, staring up into his face. I do this every time Boss goes back into a changing room. I'm glad I'm making him feel uncomfortable. He's spoilt my life, as I knew it, time for a little payback. And just to keep it straight, this is not about him avoiding my ass, this is about him planting an idea of an exit into my head. It would've been much kinder if he just went and stabbed me in the heart. Equally as comfortable.

Exit. Like I was looking for one. I was fine. I was fucking fine.

'If Boss catches you,' says Jett. 'He'll start asking questions.'

But I'm quicker than Boss. I'm quicker than most people. I get it. I let it go. I move on. Just like that. Like a snake. Like Princess. She gets it, too, she knows this here now is the best life can offer. She needs no Jett coming over oh so fucking important, offering her *exit*. Princess and me, we don't need no hero, no knight in shining armour to come and rescue us.

'Do you have this in emerald?' Boss waves a sparkling white shirt at a young shop assistant. 'Eh? What other colours do you have it in; do you have it in emerald?'

'I'm not sure,' says the shop assistant. 'I think we may have it in blue. And chocolate.'

'Tell you what,' says Boss. 'How about you bring me the shirt in all the colours, eh, how about that?'

'Like I already said, sir,' the shop assistant drawls on, plain oblivious to Boss's rising bile. 'We only have it in two more colours. I think.'

'I suggest you stop thinking, boy, and just do as I ask.'

'Yes, sir.' The boy moseys away, like he has all the time in the world at his disposal.

'Disrespecting little son of a bitch!' says Boss. 'How am I supposed to keep *au currant* with the world of fashion if it insists on employing amateurs? If I'm paying top dollar, I should be entitled to the best service available! Why does it have to be difficult, eh? Why do these people insist on treating me like shit stuck to the bottom of their shoe?'

I can see Boss is starting to develop that bedraggled, manic sort of look which usually means he's running out of juice. I take a pillbox out of my shorts pocket, and pick out three little blue tablets.

'I don't want the fucking pills,' says Boss. 'What I want is for people to start treating me with respect. I come here to spend my money, my hard earned mother fucking cash I worked my fingers to a bone to manifest out of thin air like a fucking magician – and what do I get in return? Eh? Disrespect. And obsolete inadequacy when it comes to treating me right, complete and utter failure to give me the honour I deserve.' Boss's voice tends to climb some serious scales when he's upset, and this time is no exception. Other customers – nice looking men and women who know very little about real life, but I bet believe they know it all – throw him a curious glance or two at first, then, as his voice advances yet another octave, drop him out of their orbit like you would a hot potato out of your greedy hand. Guess Boss is a little too much of a real life experience for them, and I'm almost proud of him right now. 'When I chose to make this wretched corner of the world my new home, I vowed to do everything I could to help make it a better place, ay! I vowed to God and to myself I'll help make this miserable country into a country worth living in! On top of which, I have brought a unique service to its residents. I contribute my own money, sweat, blood and tears to making this area a better place for all of us – and what do I get in mother fucking return? A shop assistant who doesn't even know if they have a shirt I like – the only shirt I do actually like in this mother fucking department store – in a colour that I really like, which is *emerald*, and as it happens also the colour of my mother's eyes, and she is a saint of a woman, I miss her every day, ay.'

By this point he's sounding like a very tall screaming banshee, and I'm not sure what's worse, the picture or the sound. Jett looks nervous. Another man incapable of thinking on his feet, is he. I approach Boss, and one by one, pop the tablets into his mouth, as he opens it to screech out another piece of gobbledygook. Then I take his hand and walk him into a changing room. He's still talking, but in much calmer, softer tones, courtesy of the fast-acting chemical cosh. I sit his ass on a bench, leave him to mutter to his own reflection. Outside, Jett is whispering with a couple of store detectives. He slips a few notes into their pockets, they turn on their heels and leave. I go back to standing in front of Jett, staring hard.

'I get it,' he says. 'You want me to tell you what's going on. And I would if I could. Other people are involved, okay, all we can do at the moment is keep our nerve, be patient, and be ready. So get out of my face before someone sees us and jumps to a wrong conclusion.'

Another couple of days go by. I don't think Boss has ever fully recovered from that shopping-tripping episode. He's never stopped muttering to himself, for starters. It's exhausting. I'm never sure whether he's talking to me or bantering random stuff to himself. His state of mind isn't helped by the fact that he's squeezing Princess within an inch of her life. Her utter lack of useful defence mechanism makes me feel angry sometimes, other times I imagine she's probably just in shock and so playing dead for a while, until the situation either blows over or someone dies.

Another fairly unhelpful thing for everyone involved is the overnight appearance of the young shop assistant who had so unforgivably failed to deliver the colour emerald to Boss. He's been sitting in the middle of the yard for the last forty-eight hours now, caged in his own shit, crying in a foreign language, for his mother I assume.

I went to see him this morning, found him looking none too good. Some people, they're weak. And they also burn very easily. This boy is no match for this sun, despite having been born under it. I count the blisters on his back, get to fifty-seven before he turns around and sees me squatting behind the cage. He makes a limp move to grab me, but I'm miles away before he comes even close. Not fast enough not to spy the badly scorched patch of skin between his shoulder blades split up, due to the sudden movement. The boy screams. Born in the wrong skin. What you gonna do. Should've fetched those shirts much quicker than *mañana*.

I hang around with the whores for the rest of the day. They kind of let me, these days. Boss being off his head like he is, it makes life easier for them. And once the pressure's off, once the living gets easy, people tend to go easier on one another. That's how it works. Also the reason why rich people can afford to be nice to you, even when they're stabbing you in the back. Nice may not the same as good, but it sure is better than nasty.

Nico seems especially pleased with herself, which may have something to do with the fact that she's been fucking Miki for the last week or so. I don't know how I know this. I just do. No one else does, and girls seem to think he's still her nemesis, they say all sort of awful stuff about him, which I'm sure is true. Nico just sits there, or lies in the deckchair, and takes it all in. There's one girl, Sam, think Miki got Rob to rough her up for some reason, or more likely no reason at all. So she now hates Miki, although strangely enough I saw her getting quite cosy with Rob, despite all the vile things he had inflicted upon her ass. Anyway, she just won't stop going on about Miki being a bastard and a wanker, and the rest. I wish she'd shut the fuck up already, because I'm starting to experience a sixth sense that something bad would happen to her if she doesn't.

Then yesterday she jumped off the truck that picked the whores off the roadside at the end of their shift, and made a beeline for the table – without showering, or brushing her teeth first, which is pretty disgusting, even by my own standards. She sat next to Grulla, the newest girl on the block. Boss named her himself, a rare privilege he had so far only ever bestowed upon me. 'Don't be jealous, little Igor, it's just this girl has exactly the same slate-grey colour hair like Grullo horses, I simply must name her!' Well I wasn't about to get jealous of a girl who was named after a horse, was I. As for Gruella, which is how I prefer to call her on account of reminding me of Cruella de Vil, she seemed to like her new name. Guess this would be a perfect example of those extremely rare occasions where Boss somehow ends up creating a win-win situation for all concerned.

'What's up, bitch,' says Grulla. 'Did you get that huge dick punter between your legs again, the one you're sooo in love with?'

'Even better.' Sam pours herself a large glass of *rosado*, downs it in one. 'Come closer and listen the fuck up.' The girls close ranks. Even I prick up my idle ears. Not that I expect much of a story. This ain't the *Arabian Nights*, and Sam certainly ain't no Scheherazade. 'I was minding my own business at the High Point, looking out for punters as you do, smoking a bit of dope on account of my back still giving me a twinge after that *puto* pushed me down on them rocks, when who should I see but Miki, pulling in on that dirt track right below the High Point – you know the one?'

'Yeah I do,' says an albino whore at the back. Much in demand, she was, as only the rare ugly things can be. 'No wonder you get so little love, it's dead up there.'

'Well the next time I ain't gonna go,' says Sam. 'They can't expect me to bring in the bread if there's no bakers around to bake it, you know what I'm saying? Anyway, I watch Miki, he's now winding down the window, chatting with this local girl. I often see her down in the fields, picking them wild poppies, and I think, "Leave them be, girl, they'll wilt well before you get them home, them wild flowers they don't live well in a vase." But she's only a little girl, can't be older than twelve, still a baby fool.' I can see Nico gradually uncoil from her candy-stripe deckchair. But Sam can't see nothing, she just wants to tell her story. 'Then I guess he goes too far, he says something that spooks her, makes her bolt down the path and off into the fields. Miki jumps out of the truck, starts chasing after her, I can't believe I'm seeing what I'm seeing, but sure enough he soon catches up with her, pushes her down into the grass, rips off her dress and gives her one right there and then. She's thrashing about to start off with, then goes all limp whilst he's working away until he's done. Afterwards, he just gets up, pulls up his pants and drives away like nothing's happened. I had to go with a punter, who showed up fifteen minutes too late for my liking, so I've no idea how the girl's been left. Dead or alive, if you get my gist.'

Nobody says anything for what seems like a good long while. Eventually, Nico walks up to Sam and asks, 'Are you telling the truth, girl?' Her voice is like an icicle I wouldn't want to suck on.

Sam lights up a cigarette, plays it cool, but her hands are out there trembling for everyone to see. 'Yes I am.'

Nico sighs. 'Listen to me like you've never listened to anyone before in your worthless, pointless lives.' She checks around for spies, but all other whores are busy in the kitchen, believe they're baking a fuck-off cake for young Blake's birthday. He turns twenty tomorrow, and is walking around looking dead pleased with his life's achievements thus far. I am not sure what I may like to be doing on my twentieth birthday, but one thing's for sure, I wouldn't want to celebrate it with a smorgasbord of jolly whores, thugs and murderers. 'You are not to tell a soul about this, is that clear?' A couple of girls make disappointed noises. Nico bangs her hand against the table. 'Not a soul I said! Think about it! If anyone finds out what we know, we may as well be dead! If he's really raped that girl, we'll hear about it soon enough, right?'

'Hey!' says Sam. 'I saw what I saw!'

'Yes,' says Nico. 'And now you'd better un-see it. Trust me on this, the last thing you want to do, the last thing any of us wants to do, is to go around telling stories. Remember Bella? She told stories, and look what happened to her. Do you want to end up like Bella?' Girls shake their collective heads, a few cross themselves. 'Good. Make sure you keep that lip zipped.'

Grulla points at me. 'What about this one?'

I pretend I'm not even there, but it doesn't work. Nico approaches me, all serious face and furrowed eyebrows, like adults do when they wish to put a child off from doing something dangerous, like smoking or hitchhiking down a motorway. 'Who, Igor? Oh, Igor knows what's what, don't you, darling?'

Well I happen to hate when people call me darling. Patronise this, I think, and give her a finger.

'Okay, honey,' she says. 'Be like that. But also know this – if you get us into trouble, we will take you down with us. And that's a promise.'

'She doesn't even care,' says Grulla the Horse. 'Look at her, she doesn't give a fuck.'

'The girl's a monster,' says Sam. 'You should've seen what she did to them hounds.'

'Yeah, I heard,' says Grulla. 'She went for them like an animal.'

'Worse than an animal,' says a random girl whom I swear I've never even seen before. False witness, I presume. 'She ripped those poor dogs to shreds.'

I start growling, as soft as can be. They all exchange alarmed glances, pure overreaction of course, but hey, what's life without a little drama.

'I don't think Igor's gonna say anything to anyone.' Nico squats down next to me and low and behold cups my chin in her hand, then gently makes me look into her honey-coloured eyes. 'Bella was your friend. And they – those men – raped her, beat her, and then they killed her. She never stood a chance. But you do. So choose wisely.'

I scramble to my feet. My eyes are stinging with tears. I can barely see my way out of the courtyard, but I run anyway, crashing through a pile of lemons freshly delivered from the grove, sending them, and myself, tumbling down the hill, until I smash against the cage with the boy in it. He's on me like a zombie, grabbing my vest strap and my hair, mumbling some foreign shit in a horribly dislocated voice. I try to break free, but realise he's never going to let go of his own volition because he's got none left. Behind us, people shout and laugh. I look into his eyes, there's no boy left in there no more, only the demon of fear. My Mema always told me, 'There's no dialogue with a demon!' I reach into the cage and dig underneath the cracked skin below his shoulder blade. He screams, I scream, he finally lets go of me. I run, and never stop, until I start feeling a little unsure of myself, all alone in a campo and free from my captors. It is at this point that I turn around and start walking back.

MIKI

fucking a woman feels like crawling through a
muddy underpass
the faster you crawl the stickier it gets
it makes me think of all those men
stuck in the ditches during the first world war
look just look at them
flashing their disgusting bits at the moving traffic
monsters
the one I liked
the only one
look what they did to her
those morons
boss's army
i disposed of her body
jett couldn't do it
there were tears in his eyes
weak
i placed it at the edge of the forest
bottom of the hill
wrapped up in bloody rugs
i touched her belly
it still felt warm
but then i felt them coming

hill people
i tried to unfasten her ankle bracelet
she didn't need it any more
my fingers turned numb
another girl may enjoy it
a gift
get off she spoke
trees started to sway
roots began to groan
i ran

WHY ARE WE HERE?

As luck would have it, Boss is still far away with the fairies when I sneak back in the house. The air in the great room reeks of stupor, I can barely stomach it. And how do you open the windows around here. I spy a remote control in his hands, and it all comes flooding back to me, well sort of. As sneakily as I can, I pry the remote control out of Boss's rubber-spider fingers, push a random button. Nothing. And again. His *El Español Mexicano* tape kicks in, loud as fuck and equally perplexing. I push the same button; the tape goes off. *Gracias a Dios*. But listen to this; Boss is learning Mexican because he wants to move to Latin America and start a cartel. Like they don't have enough of their own. He seems dead set on the idea, too. Guess he doesn't have a home, either, but unlike yours truly, he's still looking. It's almost endearing. I decide to push one more button before giving up. *Et voilà*; the glass panes sink into the floor, leaving only a handful of twinkling stars between me and the vast expanse of the Universe. Finally, a good enough reason to feel insignificant and forlorn. I climb into my bed, lie on my side and watch the skies. My body's tired, but my mind won't quit. It's searching,

I know it is, it's searching for something tangible, something that would act as a guarantee for its survival in this life, in this world, in this body, now and forever more. Old habits die hard. Fuck you, reptile brain.

I feel a tiny movement, tucked just behind my head, and deadly familiar. Princess! I brace myself for a bite, annoyed I didn't check the bed, annoyed at the stupid snake, for slithering onto other people's territory like she owns it.

But the bite never comes. Instead, Princess glides across my shoulder and settles her long body into a coil right in front of my belly button. Well how about that for a spot of spooning.

I'm not sure what wakes me, but it comes with a ready-made feeling of dread served straight up, no frills and no fuss, certainly no fried potatoes on the side; nothing to disguise the terrible glassy taste in my mouth. The taste of fear. I know it so well, all I can do is get on with my day, right, which in this case means getting up, then being shouted at by Boss to get the fuck back into bed and wait there until he returns. I do as I'm told, thinking horrible things in my head, calling him this name and another, all the while cautious not to squash the snake.

So I lie there, watching the new morning dawn. The sun creeps up and bleeds all over the jagged mountain edge, making it look like a mouth of a freshly fed vampire. I wonder what the Hill People are up to, providing they even exist. I wonder what became of that poor baby whore with a pretty bracelet around her ankle. I'd really like it if someone, Jett maybe, came in right now and told me they know for a fact that the Hill People saved and nursed her back to health. That would be a useful thing to know, right now. I need a pee and would most definitely consider peeing all over my bed as a sign of a protest, except it's Pearl who cleans Boss's house and try as I might, I can't make myself mess it up for her. And this has nothing to do with the stupid promise I made to Jett.

Jett who, anyway?

I hear the door click down the hall and make the surliest, brattiest face I can manage without bursting out laughing.

'Igor!' Jett rushes into the room, as if chased by a pile of lemons. I promptly drop the face. Crap oh crap. Hopefully he didn't notice. 'You look just like I feel. Come on, we don't have much time!'

But I'm already out of the bed. I catch an odd look in his eye, the look that makes my pussy feel nice and warm inside out. I remember I'm only wearing my sleeping knickers, basically a pair of boy's shorts I made Boss buy for me during one of our shopping expeditions. This could look bad, hope Jett's not stupid enough to think I'm sleeping with Boss.

'Are you sleeping with–'

I stamp my foot, as hard as I can.

'No,' he says. 'Of course not. Listen, Igor, the shit's hit the fan and the place is crawling with the police. A local girl never made it home, she was only eleven, so they're keen to interview all potential witnesses.

The rumour has it that Miki went too far–'

I stamp my foot again.

'You already know? How? Never mind; but if you know, then others must know about it too.' He falls silent for a moment. 'This is not good news.' I stamp my foot again. 'What?'

I pass my fingers over my throat and cock my head, waiting for an answer.

'I fear she's dead, yes. Miki would never leave a witness.'

More silence.

When I was growing up, our classes were regularly interrupted by a minute of silence every time a politician died. It was meant to be a sign of respect, even though none of the pupils gave a shit, the teacher didn't give a shit, my parents didn't give a shit, and as for me, well I stopped giving shit long before any of them did, and on far more accounts than a death of a politician who also happened to be a Second World War hero and the Father of the Nation. How many fathers can a nation possibly have. Besides, what's up with all the silence. I may not speak or feel much, but I still know that grief isn't silent. It's violent and piercing, it's raging, and quite frankly too gruesome for words. I saw it on *Survival* once, there was this rogue lion terrorizing an African tribe, helping himself to their goats and chickens, so when this baby boy disappeared, his mum knew straight away the lion took it, and she threw herself onto the ground and started to wail and rub dust into her eyes until they bled... Okay, maybe I invented that very last bit, but the rest stands. And as for the dead girl, well I don't see why Jett should feel so upset; I mean it isn't like he hasn't seen it before. It isn't like she's any better than Bella, and Bella suffered a fate far worse than this stupid little brat. What the fuck was she thinking, walking all by her lonesome through a whore and pimp-infested land. I reckon she got exactly what she deserved, and the same goes for her parents, letting her roam around Boss's country with no submachine gun to keep her company. 'But right now, we must remain focused. If this operation goes well, it would spell the end for Boss, and we hope the end of the corrupt political structure that enabled his, and others similar operations to go on. We can't afford to lose Boss to a rape or murder charge.'

Bored now. And in need of a pee. I don't really give a fuck about Jett's agendas, I'm only listening because he's sexy, and I hope to sleep with him one day soon. And the sooner the better, because he's starting to get on my nerves. Why do men feel like they have to talk all the time, the world would be much better place if they'd only let their, hmm let me see – cocks do all the talking. Except when it came to men like Miki. Who should've been castrated at birth, then – oh I don't know, can't think straight, Jett is distracting me. Maybe I'll turn this into a graphic novel one day, when I have more time to think. And also learn how to draw.

'Did anyone see Miki do it?'

I finger-write SAM in the air.

'Mum?'

I shake my head, write SAM again, this time slower.

90

Jett frowns. 'Ham?'

Beautiful but illiterate, as well as police-style dumb. Think I could live with that.

I write SAM again, this time letter by letter.

'Sam.' His jaw clench, in an extremely manly way. 'Does Nico know?'

I write YES.

'You could just nod, if that's any easier.' Jett smiles/ Igor melts. 'Good. Knowing Nico, she's probably put a fear of God into Sam. She'll keep schtum alright.' He checks his watch. 'Police have been questioning Boss for a while now, I need to go back before they notice me gone.'

I'll notice you gone.

'So this is where you come in, Igor. I've taken Pearl into the campo – you know that old well to your left, just after you enter the main gates of the lemon grove? She's hiding in a makeshift shelter about half a kilometre to the west. I need you to get a few provisions down to her, make sure she's okay, hang around for a while, make sure she doesn't panic and do something stupid. I'll be there just after dark, and take it from there. What do you say, Igor? Can I count on you?'

I walk down campo way, kicking the pebbles off my path, trying not to breathe in the dust. I hate promising people stuff, because they always expect you to deliver, and I find this kind of naiveté on their part not only boring but also kind of offensive. I carry a heavy bag: food supplies to tide Pearl over until Jett comes to the rescue. I spent ages creeping outside the kitchen window, waiting for the chance to jump in and grab a few things – a two-litre bottle of water, a bunch of bananas and a tin of sardines in olive oil. Scraped my shin making an exit – as wounds go I've seen worse, but it still stings like a mother fucker. And I keep thinking a fly may land on it, which is one of those thoughts that instantly make me lose my cool. It occurs to me I forgot the tin opener. I drop the bag on the floor and dig out the tin, take it out of the box. There's a mini tin opener inside. Thank fuck for that, hate to think I bust my gut for a job only half-done.

Never a good thing, thoughts. They make an already messy situation even messier, and a good situation, if there's ever such thing, bad. Wonder what Pearl must be thinking. Hopefully she's realising just how stupid she is. Getting herself pregnant like that. Like a moron. Well, I hope she enjoys her own company, because I ain't sitting in that hole with her for love nor money – not that anyone's paying me for this, although I think they bloody well should. Besides, Boss will need me back in the house when he returns from his salvage mission, he'll want me around to soothe and reassure, like the angel of mercy that I truly am.

'What a horrible waste of my precious time,' he told me, upon his return from police interrogation. 'A child's gone missing. What's that got to do with me, eh?'

I pretended I know nothing. Which wasn't difficult. Having been interrogated by the police didn't exactly improve the state of Boss's general mental health. He kept telling me how badly they had treated him, how disrespectful they had been towards him and all that he represents, on and on he droned in that hurt, walled-off manner addicts develop as a way of coping with their daily misery. I don't know any addicts, as such, but somehow I recognise the feeling. Don't ask me how, I just do.

'The good news is,' he continued, 'at this stage they still believe she's only missing, so we have time to bury the evidence before the evidence buries us.' That's alright then. Boss loosened up his tie. 'These clothes are suffocating me. I need to get into something comfortable, ay.' He took off his white linen suit and candy-stripe silk shirt. 'Get me my *Traje corto*!'

Traje Corto was his current favourite item of clothing, a tight fitting suit, ideally worn by the male flamenco dancers. 'This one is very special, my little Igor,' Boss had told me. 'It was worn by Carmen Amaya, the untamed child of that most feral of all races – she was a *Gitana*, ay, she danced like death itself, raging against life, and she danced like life, lusting after death; she was the tender hereafter and the ravages of hell, all tangled up in the one last dance. And every dance she danced, it was her last. I had it adjusted, of course. She was small, like a bird. In fact, I think she looked a lot like you, Igor, look.'

He showed me a couple of old photographs of this Carmen Amaya, and of course she looked nothing like me. What she did look like was a) an angry man, and b) a praying mantis, prowling about the stage with a single objective; to tease the real nature out of her adoring male audience. According to Boss, it wasn't at all unusual for her to put her foot right through the stage when she was dancing, so I guess she didn't like what she got out of them. Maybe she got nothing back. A terrible thing, showing yourself for who you really are, giving your all, then getting nothing in return. I almost feel sorry for the poor old Carmen, but not quite. You need to realise when you're barking up the wrong tree, know when to quit. She never did, and now she's dead, and it's all her own fault.

I helped Boss enter into his pristine white pleated shirt and waistcoat, then buttoned up the two upper buttons on his trousers – my least favourite order of this day so far. It was too hot for the jacket, he said, but still insisted I tied the scarf around his fat waist. He looked like a right dick, pacing the floor, half-dressed up as a woman flamenco dancer who liked wearing man's clothes.

'All the pussy they could eat. And what do they do? They rape and kill a little girl. Ay, ay!' He beat his chest with both clenched fists. 'And there's nothing I can do to make it right. Miki has connections. I knew something was wrong with that boy the moment I laid my eyes upon him – but his people, they have border connections, they are precious to us. They tricked me into taking him on, ay, played me for a fool. And now I'm having to protect him, cover up for his godawful crime.' He dropped down to his knees, the best he could in such tight attire, and lifted his head up towards the ceiling. 'As Igor is my witness, I will avenge the death of that little girl. Sooner or later, Miki will pay for what he's done, I won't rest until he does.'

Not if I get there first.

Fuck sakes. How about I kill all of them, just for getting on my nerves. And also for generally standing in my way. Not that I'm going anywhere, as such, but it's the principle that counts.

I open the gates and enter the lemon grove. A stray dog appears and starts baring his teeth at me. I give him a look, and he stops. Jett said west, which sounded self-explanatory at the time. I look at the sun, high up in the sky. Strange to think that something so distant can still burn a hole in the Earth-boy locked up in a cage. I wonder what the sun would have to say about us, if it could talk. I wonder how the human race rates amongst all the other weird and wonderful stars and stripes in the Universe. I bet everyone hates us – I know I do.

Okay; my spidey senses are telling me to go left. I proceed on my not very merry, aware of that stray following me at a safe distance. Stupid animals, always searching for a new master.

After about ten million minutes I stop by the old well. Mema had a well in her yard. It had a proper little brick house built above it, painted bright white, its flat roof covered in a jungle of lush jade-coloured moss. Inside, there was a spool with a rope neatly wound around it, and a wooden bucket tied to its end. A large wheel lowered the bucket all the way down to the underground spring, and pulled it out filled with the lovely cool water. It took ages for me to grow big enough to be allowed to handle the wheel, and even then only under Mema's eagle-eyed supervision.

'Go away, Mema,' I said. 'I'm not a baby.'

'Exactly,' she said. 'Only big girls know how to follow instructions. Babies, they only know how to whinge.'

'I never whinge, Mema, do I?'

'Never.'

'But my sister does, because she is a stupid little baby; isn't she, Mema?'

'Even if that were true, it's hardly becoming for a young lady of your calibre to call people names. Especially your own sister.'

'I'm not a young lady, though, am I, Mema?'

She laughed. 'No, I don't suppose you are.'

'So did you just lie to me, then?'

'Yes I did. I forgot who I was talking to, and I apologise.'

'That's alright, Mema. So what am I, then?'

'You're just – you.'

'But is that good, just being me?'

'Oh yes.'

'I'm too good to call my sister stupid?'

'That also.'

'Even though she is?'

Mema clapped her hands. 'Okay, listen up, and listen good; hold that wheel with your right hand and take the hook off with your left.' I do as I'm told. 'Now hang the hook on that nail over there, that's right. Careful, the hook is no longer helping you stop the wheel from running wild. Holding with both hands, let the wheel unwind anticlockwise, slowly does it.' I followed her instruction with eager determination. And it paid off. 'You are a very good pupil. You may even get a treat afterwards.'

'What treat, Mema?'

'Later. Now, you concentrate.'

'Can I go to the ice cream parlour on the corner, and get two scoops, vanilla and chocolate, and can I walk on my own because I'm now in charge of the well?'

'We'll see. First, you need to get the water out of that well. Finish what you started. Otherwise nothing will ever get done.'

One of my last memories of Mema is of her climbing inside the little house above the well, like she did every springtime for as long as I could remember. I was about to turn sixteen, and my life was too hectic for words, so we kind of lost touch. Even though this was hardly my fault, I had enough grace to vow that I would make it up to her, as soon as I had enough free time to do it properly. And in the meanwhile, I decided to do my best to avoid her.

'Hello, Spiderwoman!' I strolled over, feeling slightly embarrassed it was her balancing precariously above the deep dark chasm, and not me – even though it had always been her. No one else was allowed to participate in the annual whitewashing of the well's belly. Mema only trusted herself with this job. 'Would you like some help?'

'No,' she said. 'You have better things to do with your life than help an old woman.'

This made me angry. 'You're not an old woman, Mema! You'll never be an old woman, so don't say such a thing.'

'And when did you become the one who tells Mema who she is? Or what she can say, or do? Eh? When did you become the shaman?'

'I just–'

'Yes – *just*! Because *just* is what you do, isn't it? So naturally *just* is what life gives back to you.' Mema gave me a long hard stare over her rimless glasses. 'How did you grow up to be so picky?'

Sometimes Mema wasn't very nice to me.

Back on the planet Lemon Grove, I feel an irresistible urge to peer over the edge of the well in front of me. I creep up, afraid I may slip and fall into something as horrible as a snake pit, wishing I brought Princess with me for protection. Just imagine, a pit of regular snakes slithering towards me, tongues a-flicker and fangs dripping with venom, but then out of nowhere, the mighty king cobra springs to my rescue, and the mere sight of her is enough to disperse the ugly mob. Somewhere behind me, the stray dog whimpers. I look back, find him caught up in a state of limbo that stupid dogs so often get stuck in, pushed forth by the nature that commands them to stay near their human, whilst simultaneously pushed back by the survival instinct telling them to quit getting themselves into trouble on account of blindly following the blind. I watch the silly beast tiptoe forward an inch or two, then scramble back behind the lemon tree. One step forward, two steps back. And again. A cat would rather die than be seen behaving like this.

I draw closer to the edge of the well. The ground is cracked by tons of sunshine bearing hard upon its face, with the fractures going as deep as the eye can see. I try not to think what lives in those cracks. I'm starting to feel annoyed again, this time with this whole project. Especially the part where I got involved. What was I thinking. Stealing supplies, lugging them around campo in this heat, searching for a wrongly impregnated girl who should've known better; being followed around by a mad dog with a missing left fang, and finally peering over the edge of a deserted well, because it reminds me of something long gone that's never coming back, and just as well it ain't.

At first, all I can see is a dusty brown gloom, but soon my eyes adjust enough to make out a cage, stuck I'd say halfway down towards the centre of the Earth. A dark outline inside the cage brings all the speculation about what had become of the young shop assistant to an abrupt end. Must admit, I wasn't that far off beam, with my stakes placed high on him being buried alive, albeit in a grave much shallower than this one. As I move to leave, I glimpse a movement inside the cage. Or at least I think I do. Probably just my imagination, or it could be the sun, playing dirty tricks with my mind. Keep on walking Igor, or whatever my name is.

I find Pearl asleep under the only orange tree amongst the lemons. How did this happen. I mean, did they plant it there on purpose, or did a bird drop an orange pip as it flew over the grove. And do birds even bother with oranges. Has Pearl chosen it because it was different, or did she just go and slump up in the first shade available. One thing I know for sure, if she has a daughter, I think she should call her Orangina.

The stray dog's still with me, snarling and salivating over Pearl. Bet he'd eat her if he could. So much for the man's best friend. I never had one. The best friend, I mean. I don't know why, maybe for the lack of trying. What's the point of having anything if you first have to kill yourself trying to get it. Pearl stirs. She turns out to be one of those people who wake up knowing where they are straight away, none of that sleepy *where am I* look, none of that drowsy confusion. Maybe this comes with the territory; maybe whores learn how to sleep with one eye open, in case they miss a punter or indeed a trick.

'Did you bring water?'

I throw her the bag. Did I bring water Who does she think I am, a stupid. Hardly worth wasting my imaginary question marks on, this girl. Pearl drinks for a long time, without spilling a drop. Sleeps with one eye open, never spills a drop. People, and especially women, are rarely that neat. Wonder if she's had any military training in her previous life. North Africa girls, they're all, like, *Vive Liberte* and shit, so I wouldn't be at all surprised if Pearl was once a toy-soldier. Seems like a pretty solid story to me, I just need to work out why she's left the army and the quest for freedom in order to pursue a career that could hardly be more different, and then I have myself another graphic novel in the making.

Except the fact that I found Pearl asleep under the tree and not in the shelter makes my story sink like a rock. She ain't no soldier. A real soldier would never risk their life for a bit of fresh air. Enough stories. My job here is done. I start walking back, feeling as tired as can be, not to mention breathless as fuck. I must remember to ask Boss to get me a treadmill, get fit for the boys and whatnot.

'Hey!' I hear Pearl calling after me. I don't stop. 'Girl!'

God, what an annoying voice you have given her. I'm not answering to that, I will just keep on keeping on instead.

'Igor! Stop!' Pearl crops up right in front of me, like a little mushroom after an autumn downpour. 'Where is Jett?'

I shrug. Pearl looks pleasingly dishevelled, her hair hanging around her face like a heavy cloud made out of yellow candyfloss, her eyes bloodshot and puffy, as if she tried to cry them out of their sockets, maybe so she could no longer see her terrible predicament. And yep, I think her predicament is terrible. If I were her, I would just go ahead and kill myself. Looking at Pearl, however, I doubt she has suicide on her mind. On the contrary, she seems hell-bent on demanding stuff from life, must be the pregnancy kicking in, or perhaps she was born that way. I can feel anger rising in my chest.

'But he is still coming, yes? Igor? Jett is coming to take me to his people?'

I shrug again. Like I said, my job here is done. I want to go back to Boss and eat watermelon and sweetmeats and sleep in my silky soft bed, and chat to my best friend Princess. I barge my way past Pearl, but she won't leave well alone. She grabs my arm, and yanks the rest of me to a halt. So much stronger than she looks, perhaps she works out whilst she's waiting for clients. Or her strength's down to having a lot of sex with a lot of different men, maybe this produces results well above and beyond the reach of any other, more ordinary fitness regime.

I growl, and this time I mean it.

'You must know something, girl! Tell me what you know! Speak to me!'

I'm not very strong, but I'm fast. I kick the side of her left ankle, catch it off-guard, and at the same time I push hard against her shoulders. She trips up like a good girl, and falls backwards into a gentle ditch shaped like a child's grave. I hold onto her clothes, a little, just so she doesn't exactly crash-land and start miscarrying her stupid baby. But once she's hit the ground, I start walking and only turn around to look at her once.

THE SHOP ASSISTANT

Mother lowers Felizio down on the kitchen floor before looking out of the window. Felizio moans, like he does every time he is away from mother's breast, or he does not have a chocolate biscuit smeared all over his chubby face. I am glad he was born, but I don't like the fact that my mother is also his mother now.

She is looking out of the window again, peering down at the evening shadows, which all look like me at first. Felizio is crying and pulling at her skirt. Mother gets a chocolate bonbon out of her pocket and shoves it into his hand. Her eyes remain glued on the street below. I am nowhere to be seen.

BEWITCHED

Nina was my worst nemesis ever. And, believe it or not, I had a few. But no one got to me as bad as Nina. Small and perfectly formed, she commanded the playground with one flicker of her velvety lashes. She had girls queuing to comb her silky brown locks before *and* after school, and boys helping her negotiate puddles and railway tracks. Teachers not only adored her, but entrusted her with those extremely important missions, like fetching forgotten lunches from their home, or ensuring we're all properly lined up before our trip to the museum. She wrote brilliant stories à la Agatha Christie, she sang like a dirty little angel that's been rolled in honey and sprinkled with rose petals. She added and multiplied like a town hall accountant, and she ran like a gazelle. Basically, everybody was more or less secretly in love with her, including myself. We spent all our free time together, sitting on the sandy river embankment, riding our bikes along the dirt tracks though sunflower fields, and climbing wild cherry trees on the hill overlooking the rest of the world.

I was happy.

'Nina is my best friend ever,' I told Mema. 'We shall never ever part.'

'Wow,' said Mema. 'That sounds like a very special friendship.'

'Special. Yes. And tomorrow we'll prick the tips of our index fingers with a tiny needle and then we'll mix our blood so hers runs in my veins, and mine in hers, and then we'll call ourselves Blood Sisters.'

'Just like a fairy tale.'

'Exactly, Mema. This will be our own fairy tale.'

I wasn't talking your run-of-the-mill Hans Christian Anderson and Brothers Grimm; I was talking the real fairy tales, spoken straight out of a belly of the beast, human and otherwise, filled with blood and gore, the ones where Prince Charming doesn't bring Sleeping Beauty out of her slumber with a kiss, but a good old fuck. My dad bought me an entire collection of the Real Fairy Tales for my ninth birthday, all six large shiny hardcover tomes, one for each continent. The only continent missing was Antarctica, which I always felt was a bit of a pity. I felt Antarctica could tell a good story, given chance.

The next day I met Nina underneath a giant poplar tree at the back of our school, as arranged, and pricked my finger, as arranged – which by the way was quite a traumatic thing for me to do on account of being terrified of needles – but when it was her turn, Nina flatly refused to do it.

'But Nina,' I said. 'You promised.'

'So?'

'Promises are meant to be kept.'

'Says who?'

I had to stop and think. 'Me.'

'Well, I guess I'm not you.'

As I watched Nina gather her stuff, I suddenly felt this terrible nameless sensation rise from the pit of my stomach, putting every other emotion I had experienced up to this point to shame. Without really planning to, I said, 'Please don't go.'

Nina looked down on me. 'I'm not hanging with you any more! You're just too weird, plus you're a show-off and I hate show-offs.'

'No I'm not,' I managed to say, despite the strange lump in my throat. 'Why are you being so bloody horrid?

'That's another thing,' she spat. 'You talk like a hillbilly. Your dad's supposed to be a professor; couldn't he teach you how to speak properly?'

I pressed my shoulder blades against the tree bark until it hurt. 'Why are you being so horrible to me?'

'Because I can.' Nina dabbed her luscious lips with a pink-tinted gloss. 'And because I like it.'

'Please,' I say. Again, the words tumbled out of my mouth all by themselves. 'Don't leave me.' The minute I heard myself say this, the tension dispersed. I jumped to my feet, and I started to laugh. 'Fuck off!' I told the nameless sensation. 'Fuck off!' I told Nina. Apparently I then went on to punch her. All I can remember is feeling really good inside, even as the teachers dragged me off towards the staffroom.

'But why did she do it, Mema, why did Nina turn so nasty?'

'Some people are just made that way,' Mema said. 'Nice on the surface, but rotten to the core. They can't help it.'

'Like the flesh-eating plants,' I said. 'Pretty and pink on the outside, but if a fly comes a bit too close, snap! They swallow it up, and that's the end of that fly.'

'Did you see that on *Survival*?'

'Yes I did. At first I thought oh no, not the boring old plants, but when I saw what they got up to I became really interested. Do you think we can get one, please, Mema, maybe for my birthday? I turn eleven next month, did you know?'

She laughed. 'With friends like Nina, who needs a flesh-eating plant, eh?'

'But she is not my friend any more, which means she can never be my friend again.'

'Never?'

'Never, Mema. I hate her guts and I always will.'

As I watch Pearl lying in that ditch, I suddenly realise that she is a spitting image of Nina. Except of course for her dark skin and bright yellow hair. I know they are not the same exact person, I'm not that crazy, and yet I find it hard to look at Pearl and not see Nina. No wonder I hated her guts from the very first moment I laid my eyes on her – and now I know why.

Nina got killed by stray shrapnel, by the way, which sliced off a portion of her pretty head so skilfully that she still managed to walk and talk for hours afterwards, until some kind soul decided it was time to put her out of her misery by sending a bullet through the remainder of her brain. I was sorry to hear that. She was my arch-nemesis, after all. I got used to having her around, she was such a good person to hate, and now she was gone forever. I almost wished she'd come back to haunt me, but then

I quickly changed my mind. Having an imaginary fight with your arch-nemesis is one thing; fighting with her ghost, on the other hand, well, some things are best left alone.

'Do not go!'

I hesitate, only for a moment and only so I could properly regret turning around for the one last look, but a moment of hesitation is all it ever takes.

'Igor! Do not leave me! Please! Please, come back!'

The story of a role-reversal. Elegant or what. I stop and stand there for a while, looking down at my feet. The problem is, I can't really see them, because my eyes are stinging with tears so hot I fear they might actually blind me. The stray dog comes up to me and howls. I find this whole situation highly unbearable. Maybe this is what Kundera meant by the Unbearable Lightness of Being. Except why did he use the word lightness where the word darkness would've sufficed, I'll never understand. What a total fuck up. What a shame.

I help Pearl to her feet, even dust her down a bit, trying hard not to hit her at the same time. We walk back to the shelter, which is no more than a hole with a row of planks arranged over the top, and covered with dried-up mud and sticks and shit. Pearl seems reluctant to go in, so I decide to jump in first, show her there's nothing to fear but fear itself. Whoever said this – and by the way I remembered only the other day it was the thirty-second President of the United States, Franklin D. Roosevelt, and yeah I just happen to be an expert on the useless stuff, *and* there is plenty more where this came from – obviously never had to enter a dodgy-looking rabbit hole most probably full of deadly vipers, hairy spiders and highly animated skeletons armed with swords. But no sooner had I jumped into the shelter then I shot out of it.

'I tried to go in, just like Jett said,' says Pearl. 'But it is too hot, like inside a dragon's belly.'

So what now. I scratch my head. Stray, which is the name I accidentally gave the dog, scratches his. Pearl scratches her mini-belly. I walk back to the orange tree. They follow. It's like a scene from a silent movie. I inspect the fruit hanging off the branches.

'They are not good,' says Pearl. 'Seville oranges, very bitter. Only good for making marmalade.'

I wake up with a nice long stretch. Where's that Princess, I start feeling around the bed, except of course this is not my bed, it's the earth and burnt out tufts of grass underneath the only orange tree in the lemon grove. I open my eyes, prepared for any eventuality, but all seems peaceful beyond belief. Pearl's curled up next to me, fast asleep. Her colouring reminds me of a brown-and-yellow marshbird of South America's swamps. I'm not really into birds, especially not the dull little ones, I guess this one just happened to catch my eye with its totally show-off golden chest.

Stray is sleeping next to Pearl, his body coiled in an almost identical shape. I miss Princess, and wonder how she's doing, with all the extra comings and goings that follow rape and murder of a child. And where the fuck's Jett. I don't remember signing up for a spot of babysitting. I have places to be, people to see. He should've been here by now. I feel the all too familiar sense of foreboding mounting in the middle of my chest. Something isn't right here.

I jump to my feet. Stray jumps to his. Pearl gets up, too, then grabs my arm to steady herself. I move away. The anger's back. God I hate this girl. This whole thing, her predicament and mine, it's all her fault. Needy people, hate how they make you feel like you owe them a rescue, when it's actually them who screwed up and created the situation in the first place. And now they expect *you* to make the situation disappear – God, how I hate those needy bastards.

I watch the shadows melting into the yellow dirt. The sun's officially gone way downtown by now, and I need to be getting back, or I swear Boss will set those fucking dogs on me again. The way he's been slipping and sliding inside his so-called mind for the last couple of weeks, I'm not entirely sure he'd be able to protect me from himself, if such a need ever arises.

Pearl and I eat the last couple of bananas. Stray eats the peels. What a little pig. I would like to kick him for being so undignified. I would like to kick Pearl, too, for being stupid, as well as other, more intangible crimes she has committed against humanity. And when I say humanity, I mean me. I don't kick either of them in the end, because kicking involves a physical contact and the only physical contact I can bear is the leathery accidental one I share with Princess. Also, a distant rumble I identified as thunder a couple of minutes ago, suddenly returns with a vengeance.

'Motorbike!' says Pearl. 'It is Boss; he has found me!'

Me fucking me. I grab her arm and drag her sorry ass towards the shelter. But it's way too late. The motorbike's already on top of us.

I turn around, ready to face whatever's coming with as much attitude as I can muster. Pity I no longer speak, because if I did, I'd say, 'What took you?', or something equally cool. But on the inside, I feel disappointed. What's that all about. Like there was ever going to be a happy ending to this, any of this. Frankly, I'm disappointed with myself for feeling disappointed.

'Watch out!' Pearl pulls me backwards, into the hole and out of the bike's marauding way. I hit the ground hard; how many rock bottoms can you reach in one lifetime. I peer over the edge, just in time to see the bike parking itself into the orange tree with a mighty bang and a scream.

'It is Sam!' says Pearl. 'We must help her!'

We must what now.

I tag along, but only because I want to.

'I'm alright!' Sam shouts over to us.

'*Alhamdulillah*!' says Pearl. '*La ilaha illa Allah*!'

Come again.

We find Sam covered in dirt, but no visible injuries as such, and busy making friends with Stray. 'Who's a good boy? You are! Aren't you a good boy? Yes, you are!' Stray's tail is going like a broken metronome; he can barely keep his feet on the ground with excitement. And I thought I was his favourite.

'What are you doing here?' asks Pearl.

I check out the bike. It's one of those cross-country jobs, tough as fuck and still pretty much intact, despite the bumpy landing. I pick it up and start the engine.

'Don't,' says Sam. 'You may hurt yourself.'

'Why are you here, girl?'

Sam isn't listening. She's still fixed on me, pretending to be concerned about my wellbeing, but really only stressing about the bike. Like she's afraid I'm gonna steal it. As if. I can't do shifters. Why do things have to have gears.

'Girl!' Pearl grabs Sam's shoulders and gives them a mighty shake. 'Why you here?'

Sam tries to push her away, but Pearl won't budge, and is holding onto Sam's arm like it's a holy relic instilled with the magic power to save pocket-sized black whores from every calamity imaginable.

Stray, no longer the centre of attention, snarls through gritted teeth, his mean little eyes firmly set on Pearl. I see his shoulder blades lift and his neck pull in, and I know he's about to launch a no-holds barred attack. I've met dogs like him in the past, whenever I rode my pushbike too close to their nesting grounds in my so-called home town. Those long summer afternoons had to be filled with some half-meaningful activity, besides reading comic books and swimming across the river like ten times in a row, otherwise I'd soon start to feel like a piece of meat stuck in a pressure cooker, lid firmly on. Getting a pack of strays to chase you, then just about dodging their growling weeping jaws snapping at your heels may not sound like much to people from those more interesting parts of the world, like New York or, I don't know, Jerusalem. But growing up in a place totally devoid of any consequence did have the advantage of forcing you into becoming a creative whizz when it came to inventing brand new kicks, so eat my dust, New York errrrr Yankee.

'Have you been teasing those railway strays again?' Mema would ask, seeing me arrive home looking traumatised yet triumphant.

'I did, Mema, and I won!'

'Just remember,' she would then go. 'It's unkind to tease.'

'But it's fun, Mema! I can't wait to do it again!'

I pick up a large clump of earth and throw it at Stray. He yelps and acts surprised, but I can tell he knows that I know what he was about to do to Pearl. I stamp my foot, and he backs the fuck off.

'Igor!' Sam says. 'Naughty!'

Oh what a stupid whore this one is. I walk up and stare at her. Why is she here, is what I want to know.

'Tell us,' says Pearl. 'What are you doing here? It is not an accident you crashed into our tree.'

Except it sort of was.

'Of course it's not!' Sam lights a couple of fags, passes one to me. Her sparkly pink lipstick is wrapped around the filter, but I take it anyways. 'Jett sent me.' Has she ever kissed Jett with her sparkly pink lips. I wonder. 'He won't be able to make it, so very sorry. It's flipping chaos up there, because now that the police have found the body, nobody is allowed to leave the house. The locals are camping on the other side of the valley with torches and pitchforks, which means we girls can't go to work or anything. Proper mayhem.'

Pearl's face grows as pale as the palms of her hands. 'But… What about me?'

'Jett said not to worry,' says Sam. 'You still get to make your great escape, right. Only with this one.' She points at me. 'Instead of Jett. Who is very sorry.'

A-Team or what. I laugh. I look spooky when I laugh, all movement and no sound.

Sam is watching me, cool as a cucumber. What is happening. Have I lost my freaky magic touch. 'Jett told me to remind you of your promise to see this through. Pearl has nobody else who can help her right now, he said, only you. Did I mention he's very sorry? Because he is.'

'I will go back,' says Pearl. 'I do not want to bring trouble to Igor, or anyone.'

'Oh, and Jett said Boss hasn't even noticed you were missing,' says Sam. 'Either of yous.'

I laugh again. Stupid Boss. My jaw hurts.

'Which, let me get this straight, means that Igor could easily hand you over to Jett's people, and sneak back into the house without Boss ever clocking she was gone,' says Sam. 'Oh and Jett gave me a map, look. It's not that far, but of course it's not as close as it looks on the map. Jett said something like an hour each way tops. Oh, and he's given me a couple of torches, here, in case you should need them.'

The campo gets as dark as a barrel of tar this side of a sunset, and walking through a barrel of tar always takes more time than you may think. I grab the torches. What I really want to do is go back to the house. But I don't. It's like I'm under some spell or something.

Pearl is looking at me like I'm some kind of minor Jesus, or whoever Jesus-equivalent may be in her world. 'Thank you, Igor. Thank you so much.'

For a moment there, I wish I was man, and I could fuck her senseless, so at least I get me some real rewards. I'm that angry.

'Jett asked me to say good girl, Igor,' says Sam. 'That's it, unless I've forgotten something. Anyway, good luck – and goodbye.'

That's just too many goods for my liking.

JETT

Corvette cuts the last sharp turn with a precision of a scalpel blade, and pulls to a halt at the far side of the clearing, nuzzling up to the very edge of the cliff.

Alejandro's leaning against the official issue black Mercedes, every bit as inconspicuous as a rabbi in a cathedral. He is too busy smoothing the creases out of his grey linen suit to acknowledge my arrival. Nothing new there. I light a Gauloises and, just for a moment, it feels good to be alive.

The next moment, the banging starts again, reminding me that life's nothing but a lying cheating bitch; no good ever comes out of courting it.

'What's with the noise?' Alejandro asks.

I shrug.

'Sounds to me like you may have a live one locked up in that boot.' Alejandro pushes his white panama hat off his forehead, wipes off the sweat with the back of his flabby hand. 'I'm sweating like a P.I.G. in butcher's shop. How can anything survive in this heat I'll never know.'

I finish my Gauloises. It sure was a pleasure.

'Sebastian, *s'il te plait*… Tell me you don't have a person locked up in that boot.'

'I don't have a person locked up in that boot.'

'*Merde*! I can't believe you brought along a body.'

'Boss says jump, you say how high.' I light another Gauloises. 'Field work, office work, they're not that different.'

'There's one big difference,' says Alejandro. 'Office work won't get you killed.'

'What about those paper cuts? I hear they can be deadly.'

'A truly smart ass would not bring a potential witness to our meeting.'

'He's already dead.'

'Doesn't sound dead to me.'

Alejandro's right. The body is making a lot of racket. Wonder if he's sensing the presence of a good cop.

'One of them?'

I shake my head. 'Civilian.'

'*Putain*!' Alejandro kicks a tyre. 'Show me.'

'Why?'

'Just show me, my friend. It's an order.'

I know precious little about relationships, but one thing I do know is that friends don't pull rank on each another. We walk over to the Corvette. I open the boot. The boy starts thrashing about like his life depends on it. I could put a stop to his hopes right here right now, wring his scrawny neck and lose his body to the ravine, but Boss wants him back alive.

'Who is he?'

'Just a boy, unlucky enough to be in the wrong place at the wrong time.'

'I need more, Sebastian. Sleepers are required to

log in every name, you know the rules.'

I slam the boot shut. The boy lets out a terrific cry, despite the well-padded gag over his mouth.

'His hand! *Merde*! Open the boot, open the fucking boot!'

Sure enough, the boy has managed to free one of his hands and stick it into harm's way. I check his fingers. Broken, every single one. 'Nothing to worry about. He's in for much worse than a few broken bones.'

'But I am worried,' says Alejandro. 'I'm worried about you, my friend.'

I look up, but Alejandro's gaze is fixed upon the horizon. 'Oh yeah?'

'Yeah.'

I light another Gauloises.

'You smoke too much.'

I laugh. 'You worry I smoke too much?'

'No,' says Alejandro. 'I worry you've been playing the field for too long.'

'We do what we do.' My mouth suddenly feels dry. I put out the cigarette and stick it behind my ear for later. 'You, me, everyone.'

'Except for the fact that when a field mole fries, things tend to spin out of control and the entire operation becomes compromised.'

'Bullshit.'

'Sebastian…'

'Bullshit.'

'It's over, my friend,' says Alejandro. 'We're pulling you out.'

'No.' I shake my head. 'We're too close.'

'This is not request, it's an order. You are to return to the camp, tie up loose ends, and meet me back here in forty-eight hours – is that clear?'

'Loose ends?'

'The pregnant whore, the dumb kid… get rid of them.'

Alejandro starts walking towards the Mercedes.

'Alejandro…'

I wait for him to fully turn around before I place a bullet into the middle of his sweaty forehead. I have never shot a man in the back in my entire career. No need to start now.

THE REAL IGOR

The map couldn't be clearer: we follow the outside boundary of the lemon grove until we reach the dry riverbed. Here, we turn left and continue for about three kilometres until we get to the iron bridge. *Et voilà*; Jett's Interpol crew – meet Pearl, Pearl – meet Jett's Interpol crew, Igor – skedaddle.

The moon's almost full, and we find it easier not to mention safer to walk without turning on our torches. Pearl's being a surprisingly good soldier, swift and silent, and almost invisible to the enemy, especially now that she's hidden her bright yellow fleece under a dark scarf. Against my own self, I approve.

'Look!' Pearl whispers. 'The bridge!'

She then does that thing the moviemakers use for creating a particularly sentimental ending, the one where after many trials and tribulations, the main character, usually a dumbass woman, drops their guard at the very last minute and rushes off towards the finishing line without remembering to look left or right, only to then get hit by a train, or a bullet, or a great white shark. I run after her, grab the back of her dress and reel her in. I even have to place my very own index finger over her lips, before she gets my gist. Seriously, am I the

120

only one with some sense around here.

'Sorry, Igor,' she whispers. 'I forgot myself.'

Well lucky you. Goddammit, I think, but to be brutally honest I'm kind of pleased with my current role of a lone superhero, forced to yet again make some tough decisions in order to save the world.

I make Pearl squat down in a craggy bush, and forge ahead on my own, as stealthy as The Phantom, aka The Ghost Who Walks. I can see the bridge pretty clearly from here, but there seems to be no rescue party awaiting us there. I creep closer, and closer still, until I'm basically on it. There's no one here, not on the bridge, or under it, not to the left of it, or to the right.

I growl.

'Shhhh,' warns Pearl. 'What did we say about keeping quiet?'

And what did I say about *not* following my ass.

We wait. I'm cold on the outside, and I'm cold on the inside. Pearl is being sick again, down beside the riverbed. We have no water left. Or bananas. If only Stray stayed with us, I could've sent him for help. But he went off chasing Sam and her bike, never to return – and who can blame him.

'I am starving.' Pearl has climbed back, looking further worse for wear. 'Makes no sense, one minute I am sick, the next I am so hungry I could eat a whole cow.'

That's only because you're:

a) disgusting, and

b) carrying a devil's child.

I really, really want to tell her this, but I don't. For the obvious reasons, none of which have anything to do with wishing to spare Pearl the truth.

I loathe analysis of any sort, but our predicament does seem pretty damn dire. I now know there's no way back, not for Pearl and not for me. My brain tells me otherwise, it says I could easily stroll back into the house, as casual as can be, and everything would be alright. Except that the rest of me just happens to know this to be a lie and that the next time I see Boss I'd better be prepared to die.

Well, I'm going to die some day, but not today I don't think. Something will happen. Something always does in the end. The Interpol people may still show up. Or Jett will appear on the horizon, take care of things so I don't have to, and bring this situation to a successful climax. Talking of which, I would really like to kiss Jett before I die. Check him out a bit, see how well we fit together.

Pearl runs down to the riverbed again. Moments later, I hear her heave. There's something seriously wrong with that woman. If she doesn't stop throwing up she will die. Or worse, miscarry. Force me to deal with all the blood and gore and tiny dead babies.

I shut my eyes, indulge in a little daydream about Pearl dying the fuck out of my life, leaving me free to do whatever I want. Can't say I'm entirely sure what that is. The jury's still out, and good luck to them.

'Igor? What do you think you're doing?'

'Mema? What are you doing here? And why do you call me Igor, that's not my name.'

'You're Igor alright,' she says. 'You have always been Igor.'

I feel the fear gripping my heart. 'No, Mema! I have a different name, you know, it's–'

'Igor. That's who you are now.'

I start crying. 'No, Mema, I'm not!'

'So if you're not Igor, who are you?'

'I'm–I'm–help me out, Mema, help me remember who I really am!'

'If your name is Igor,' says Mema. 'Then Igor is who you are.'

'Why are you doing this, Mema? I thought you loved me!'

'Love?' Mema comes closer. 'You want to talk about love?' Mema comes closer still, until she's towering over me like no Mema I've ever known could or would. 'Don't you dare talk to me about love!' She covers my mouth with a giant hand, I try to get away, but she's too strong, I try to breathe, but there's no air, I struggle and kick, to no avail.

'Igor! Igor!'

I open my eyes, just as Pearl's hand lands across my face with a resounding slap. I'm far too confused to slap her back. And also relieved to see the giant Mema gone to wherever it is the dream Memas go after being horrible to people. Then the vague yet tiresomely familiar sense of dread enters my so-called awareness. I check in with Pearl, her eyes confirm my suspicion that things are far from peachy. Which for some reason still gets to me. By now, I should be perfectly at ease with the fact that bad situations can only get worse, and good situations don't actually exist. But I'm not. Go ponder, drown yourself in a pond while you're at it.

Pearl points towards the bridge. There's a red truck parked on the opposite side of the riverbank, with a small posse gathered around it. Perhaps it's the Interpol, fashionably late in a proper European grand dame fashion, but nevertheless here to save the day.

'It is Boss's crew,' says Pearl. 'I hear different voices. He has more men, new men, looking for us.'

Well there goes hope, squished dead like a bug. The men are suddenly on the move, no time to shed no tears, or hit Pearl just because. All we can do right now is watch as they split into three groups, and spread away from the bridge, in every direction – except ours.

'*Alhamdulillah*!' says Pearl.

Just then, another truck appears out of nowhere and pulls up on the bridge. More hunters. Where did Boss manage to get all these men from so fast, a hothouse? Pearl's looking at me, ashen-faced and ready to give up the ghost. I take her hand and pull her down to the ground. She smells of sick, and also palm trees. I crush a few small clumps of earth between the tips of my fingers until all there's left is pale yellow powder. Then I do it again. Ashes to ashes, dust to dust. The birds are no longer singing. I no longer hear the wind. The moon is hiding behind a motionless black cloud. I get a feeling I've been here before, right here, right now, in this. Which seems not only seriously bloody unfair, but also goes to show just how totally out of inspiration the gods really are. A cigarette butt lands about a half a metre away from my face. It's still burning. I quickly bury it in a pile of dust. Where are the rest of the hunters then. I dare get on my knees, look around, my elbows bent and hands dangling in front of my belly like a meerkat. Every birthday photo, age one to thirteen, I struck this same pose. I don't know why. Never even saw a meerkat in those days, not even on *Survival*. Clearly:

a) I was a peculiar little kid, and

b) some things never change.

The hunters have passed us by, but I suspect they may well return in a tighter formation, rake us out like a couple of rainworms. And why oh why didn't I steal a machine gun or two out of Boss's arsenal before I left. Stupid, stupid girl, never getting anything right, never have done, highly unlikely I ever will. So God, as you sure seem to favour the survival of the stupidest of folk, how about you:

a) get my ass out of this predicament like right now, or

b) if you really truly can't be bothered, then at least get me a superstar pass through heaven's gate, you shithead. No trick questions from the gatekeepers, either, no waiting in no queue, and an immediate appointment with a plastic surgeon in case half of my head or tits gets blown off in the process of exiting this realm.

Oh fuck this.

I take Pearl's hand again, pull her up onto her knees.

'No,' she says. 'Igor. No.'

But get up she does, and she listens as I tell her that there's nothing to worry about so she can relax and let me take care of shit. I do this without making a noise, like a proper superhero who needs no sound nor fury to make herself heard.

I take a deep breath, let it all the way out, until I'm forced to gasp for another. Then I run. I run like the wind, with Pearl's hand locked in mine, never looking back, along the bank, we go slipping and crumbling down with it, hitting the riverbed hard, closing in on the bridge, interrupted only by the shouts of the huntsmen, at first surprised, soon dripping bloodlust as they gather in hot pursuit.

We manage to scramble up the other side before they start to shoot. I run to the first truck, no keys, not even spares tucked into the sun visor. Don't these peasants know anything. Don't they watch movies. I run to the second truck, open the door, and can't quite believe my eyes when I see a key already planted in the ignition, with a tasteful Playboy keyring dangling off it. I reckon I can live with that. Pearl clambers in, I jump after her and turn to close the door, but there's a smiling old man standing right in between me and the handle. I know him well; he's the only local man Boss has ever allowed to enter his inner circles. He often gave me handfuls of golden sultanas, smiling just like he is now. I turn the key, motion him to please get the fuck out of my way. He doesn't budge. I check the rear-view mirror. The hunters are advancing from every direction, not even bothering to shoot at us any more, cocksure of their victory. I reach for the door, but the old man shakes his head, ever so slowly, beaming at me like a malevolent sun. My throat tightens. Not like this, I think. Not like this.

I don't even want to look at Pearl. I hate Pearl. This is all her fault. I have failed her. I look at my feet, waiting for the men to catch up already. There's a machete on the floor. I grab it with both hands and start hacking into the old man. Don't believe he ever stops smiling, not even as he falls to the ground. I slam the door shut just as the first couple of huntsmen reach the back of the truck. I shift the gearstick into reverse and hit the accelerator, mow them down good and proper, then crash into the truck behind us so hard the impact sends it toppling down the bank. Pearl starts screaming with the thrill of it all, or perhaps because she's lost her mind to fear. Either way, she doesn't seem able to stop; she screams and screams and screams as we drive down the dirt track like a red hot bat out of a dusty hell.

WHAT HAPPENS NEXT

I drive on, down a potholed road and past the dried up Flamingo Lake. I came here once with Boss, because he wanted to hunt for snakes.

'Does Princess look sad to you, eh?' he asked. 'She looks sad to me. Sad and lonely and blue.'

Minutes later we set off, in a truck just like this one, in search for the right companion for a baby naja.

'Horseshoe snakes, ladder snakes, water snakes and grass snakes.' Boss reeled off. 'We're gonna catch them all, see which one Princess likes the best.'

I was given a pair of giant wading trousers, and boots. Boss kept looking at me, laughing. 'You look like a dolly from *Alice in Wonderland*! Ay! Don't you dare ever go changing, my Igor! I like it how you make me laugh!' Eventually, he calmed the fuck down, said, 'We will probably face a few dragonflies – just let them be, no poking, eh? They carry bad bacteria, like rabies, and I wouldn't want to end up having to shoot you. Another thing to watch out for, poisonous toads. Do not touch. Or kiss. They will not turn into a handsome prince. Stay away. Poisonous.'

We waded about the brackish water. I wasn't actually looking for snakes, except in a way of avoiding anything that resembled one, like for example sticks and long blades of water weeds. I was just passing time, sleeping on the job. Boss, on the other hand, went proper goggle-eyed, in and out of rashes and reeds he dove, waving about the butterfly net he had adapted into a snake net by the ingenious act of renaming it.

After an hour or so, he finally called it a day. 'This doesn't make any sense. This lake is usually full of flameyngos, but now they've flown off to Africa, for their summer holidays. You'd think this would be good news for snakes. You'd think they'd be ruling the roost. But no. Nature is full of mysteries, ay.' We sat on the sandy bank and had our lunch: hard boiled eggs, cornichons, fat slices of Serrano ham and bread that came out of the kitchen's wood-oven that very morning. I remember feeling as close to happy as can be, thinking to myself that – Bella's death aside – the day I attacked those dogs was definitely worth waking up to. All I had to do now was sleep and eat and follow Boss about. I had no hope or care left in the world. I felt like a proper wise old non-vegan Taoist monk, travelling the middle path of no return. 'We'll come back next autumn, you and I, go flameyngo-hunting. Romans used to hunt them for their tongues. And you know what they say, do as the Romans do, and you can do no wrong.'

Flash of nostalgia aside, I can't say I'm sorry to have missed out on the opportunity to eat a flamingo's tongue. What I do feel pissed about is this emerging sense of freedom. At least with Boss no one could ever catch me, because I was already caught.

Fuck's sake.

What have I done.

The winding track takes us deep into the cloudy mountain's side, until we hit a pile of rocks indicating the end of the so-called civilisation, not to mention the end of our escape route. I never even saw it coming, just as well I was cruising for bruising by this time. Even so, the steering wheel managed to implant itself into my ribs like a proper mother fucker. Pearl of course wore a seatbelt. I thought she was just being a pussy, but now I have changed my mind.

'The end of the road. They probably ran out of money,' says Pearl. She seems like a different woman. All bouncy and young(ish), and fear what fear. I think I prefer her terrified. But at least she's stopped chucking up. 'I am going to have a look around, care to join me?'

I think not. I open the glove compartment. And surprise, surprise, there's a gun inside, loaded and cocked, no doubt just like its previous owner. I un-cock it, it's small and tidy, will fit great tucked away into my jeans. There's a box of bullets, I'll have that too, thanks. And a packet of Marlboro Reds, I think it's about time I have me a nice leisurely cigarette.

I get out of the cab and climb onto the bonnet. Don't suppose we should hang around for too long, but I'm still going to enjoy my Marlboro Man moment, even if it kills me.

'Igor!' Pearl's face pops up next to mine, all happy and radiant and bursting with excitement. I don't think I like pregnant women very much. 'Come and see!' She grabs my hand, pulls me clear off the bonnet and appears to want to run with me, hand in hand, like we were girlfriends, accent firmly on friends, or something equally unlikely.

'Look!' She lifts the tarpaulin. 'Do you like what you see?'

I must admit that I kind of do: five giant watermelons, a basket full of eggs and a whole smoked ham, trotter still attached.

I help Pearl lift one of the watermelons. 'Drop!' she shouts, so I drop. The watermelon crashes against the hard ground and breaks into two neatest evenest halves I'm ever likely to witness a watermelon divide itself into. We sit down and start chomping and slurping until we can chomp and slurp no more. Not even after having a pee, or in Pearl's case, three.

'I've had enough.' Pearl pats the spot next to her. 'Come rest next to me.'

I don't think so, loony tune. Somebody has to organise the next leg of our race against every conceivable oddity. I start with taking the eggs and ham out of the back of the truck and depositing them on the grassy verge next to Pearl. My hands are as sticky as an overexcited cunt, hope they don't catch the fancy of a killer wasp or giant red ant. I climb back into the cab and start the engine, then fiddle around with the pain in the ass gear stick until I manage to nail the truck right on the edge of the steep side of the hill. I stop for another much deserved Marlboro Red, before relaxing the stick into neutral whilst simultaneously taking the handbrake off. I barely have the time to jump out of the cab before the truck rolls down the slope, quickly gaining momentum until it's thundering through scraggy bushes and midget trees and crashing in between rocks like a wild beast closing in on its pray, until it disappears out of my sight.

I brace myself for the sound of an explosion, but it never comes. Just as I sort of hoped. I look for Pearl, half-wondering why she didn't do anything to try and stop me, in her usual meddlesome way. I find her asleep amongst the watermelon skins. There are little red ants marching up and down her face, and I'm guessing gorging on the crusted-up juices around her mouth. Some even tramp straight in through her parted lips. Wonder what happens to them next.

I let Pearl sleep until I can barely keep my own eyes open, then give her a shake. Time to move on, Sleeping Beauty Not.

'Where is the truck?' Has to be the first thing she asks. 'What have you done, girl? How are we supposed to get away without the truck?'

Lazy or what. I hand her the egg basket; she can be in charge of something for a change. I grab the ham by its trotter, then slip down the side of the road that spells wilderness, snakes, and probably pumas – or it would do if we happen to be in the Americas. Which could well be the case.

'Where are we going? Igor? Do not leave me!' Pearl chases down after me. I can hear the eggs cracking open amongst themselves, like eggs tend to do when carried around by a careless fool. Do I really have to think of everything around here. Fuck's sake. This god of stupids sure is one very powerful god. Not only he could see straight through my attempts to hide my genius behind a cleverly disguised stupidity prayer, but has furnished Pearl with one hell of a bodyguard, i.e. me. What a shithead. Annoyed, I turn around and grab Pearl by her shoulders. She doesn't even blink, her eyes locked with mine like she has nothing to hide. I growl, softly at first, then louder and harder, baring my teeth.

'Cut it out,' she says. 'You are not a dog. You are a girl, so be a girl!'

It's not so much what she said, but the way she said it that causes my jaw to drop. The next thing I know there is a sharp 'A!' jumping out of my wide open mouth.

'That was good! See if you can do it again.' Pearl scoops out the broken eggs into their shells and hands a couple over to me. 'Raw eggs, good for your voice.'

I drink the eggs, yolks mostly. They taste fresh and salty, like oysters. I let them slip down; down all the way into the pit of my stomach. I'm not sure what's just happened, but I guess it'll come to me eventually.

I pick up my friend the ham, and we continue descending into the looming shadows of the night.

The next morning finds us curled up on a sandy bank next to the once-upon-a-time Flamingo Lake, presently devoid of both the flaming flamingos as well as water. Turns out I had put us through hours of trekking in the pitch black darkness, only to arrive to what was practically our starting point. I'm so upset, I even go and hide behind a big yellow rock to have a go at crying. I sit there for about three minutes, until there's almost a tear rolling down my cheek. But not quite. Maybe the next time I fuck up.

I wipe my dry eyes even drier and look around for any signs of an enemy approaching. But the vista remains still and unexciting, with an exception of the tall brown rock in the distance, the one Boss thought was an anthill.

'Well I never!' he proper exclaimed. 'An anthill! I always wanted to smash one of these.' By the time he returned from the truck with a mallet, however, the rock was surrounded by big sparkly dragonflies. Boss recoiled like a vampire from a cross. 'Dragonflies! Igor! Run for your life!'

Funny as this was, I was looking forward to watching Boss trying to crack open a rock. I was looking forward to imagining him in shackles, breaking stone for his sins, and maybe a few of mine, too. Happy times.

Well, no use crying over spilt milk is there. Having spent hours, days, even months of my last incarnation studying the mountain formations from Boss's place on the top of the cliff, I guess I could put some method into this madness and work out the right direction from the wrong by sitting down and thinking things through for a change.

So, turning south would lead us straight back to Boss, and even if we avoid stumbling across his headquarters, the only thing beyond it is the sea, and that's no good for us, because:

a) swimming across a river I can do. Swimming

across the sea, with a pregnant woman in tow, not so much, and

b) the coastal road is always crawling with the underbelly, like corrupt policemen (and women), as well as all sorts of villain and criminal wannabes, watching over their turf, and yours.

West is where Boss's men are searching for us, so I better not sleepwalk us into that one. This leaves us the mountains in the north, which is a clear no-go, on account of Pearl and me being sand and valley dwellers, respectively. Plus, I find mountain climbing to be one of those more puzzling of sports, treacherous to participate in and dead boring to watch, unless of course a climber loses his footing and falls down a ravine. Our last option: the mysterious east, and whatever mystical adventure awaits us there. Much better the devil you don't know always being my motto, I guess the east it is, at least until I decide otherwise. Or we run out of land. Or somebody kills us trying. Or a dragonfly gives us rabies, and Pearl and I end up murdering one another in a frothy attack of the purest rage known to man. I read a book called *Rabies* once. It was excellent, written by Borislav Pekić, a Serbian author, and better than anything that guy King has ever written. Don't recall a dragonfly ever getting a mention, but then again, I don't care to recall much.

'How are we going to cut this?' I find Pearl kneeling next to the ham, spinning it around in front of her, looking for a way in. 'Did you keep that machete?'

As a matter of fact I didn't, I left it embedded in the old man's ribcage.

'We will just have to bite into it,' she says. 'Like so.'

Pearl sinks her teeth into the ham and starts pulling off the flesh. She offers me a strip, but I politely shake my head. It's not that I think what she's doing isn't kind of neat, it's just I don't feel like being fed somebody else's half-chewed food. What's up with that. I crack a couple of eggs straight into my mouth. They taste less fresh today, doubt there's another day in the sun left in them. I crack two more, straight into my mouth, just so I don't throw them away. My heart isn't really in it, and Pearl can tell it isn't. 'You do not have to force yourself, Igor, there is plenty of ham left, look!'

I check out the sun. It's already climbed too high for my liking. We shall burn today, one way or another, and the only way for us to survive this burn is to find water. I take the ham out of Pearl's hands and swing it onto my left shoulder. We should've brought a watermelon instead.

Pearl is exhausted. Again. She's sitting on the ground, refusing to move. I want to kill that whore. Or at least leave her to fend for herself, forget all about her lazy, stupid, perfectly articulated black ass. But – allegedly – I made the bloody promise, and I'm sticking to it despite every cell in my body telling me to quit. So what's up with that.

'You go, Igor. Leave me be. I cannot keep up with you. You are strong. I am weak. I am thirsty. Bury my bones in the Sahara Desert.'

I stand there, as patient as the Grim Reaper with his hands tied, and wait for her to make up her own feeble mind on whether she'd rather live or die. If I was the Grim Reaper for real, I would take so much pleasure in dusting the souls that seemed at all hesitant. Not being sure whether you want to live or die is the worst possible option, and I should know.

'I am so sorry,' she says. 'You do nothing but help. *Astaghferullaha Rabbi min kulle zumbin wa atoobo ileh.* I seek forgiveness from Allah for all my sins and turn to Him. *Astaghferullaha Rabbi min kulle zumbin wa atoobo ileh.'*

The all of a sudden, she jumps to her feet, and wanders off into local flora like a spastic teapot.

Seriously.

What's just happened.

We take a nap underneath bony remnants of an unidentifiable tree. This must be the virgin land, untouched by people. Or if they did try and tame it, they sure have lost that battle a long time ago. There's nothing human about this place, is what I'm saying. Pointy stones, sharp turns, jagged edges and spiky thorns is what greet our every step. Pearl's pink espadrilles are useless here. At least I'm wearing my sturdy leather sandals. So glad she's like size zero and we can't trade footwear. The way I'm going with this role of playing Jesus Christ the Merry Saviour, I bet I would've given her my own shoes, left myself with nothing but a pair of bleeding bare feet.

The sound of a giant engine jolts us back from our slumber. Like a good girl, Pearl jumps to her feet and runs for cover. I run beside her, simultaneously trying to twig how the hell they have managed to find us. And how the doubly hell have they pulled off commanding anything remotely motorised across the terrain that even the mountain goats are staying well clear of, and the two of us found nigh impossible to navigate on foot. And also, what's up with my mind, going on analysing shit instead of working out how to save my ass. As a matter of fact, if these are indeed to be the last moments of my life, I'd really like my mind to shut the fuck up for once, so I can lay my burden down and feel one moment of peace before I die.

'Igor! Here!'

Pearl is standing on the edge of a hole in the ground, holding the end of a thick hairy rope. An old well. Forgive me while I recoil in horror. 'Do not be afraid. Look, I go in first.' She dives in. 'Just hold onto the rope!' I listen to the sound of an engine closing in behind me. They must've seen me by now, no point trying to dodge this bullet. 'Igor! Jump! Now, Igor, now!' Oh fuck it. I jump. And just as I'm about to dip my head below the edge, a helicopter pops up over the hill right in front of me.

A helicopter. Well someone clearly means business. I'm thinking cartel, I'm thinking Interpol, I'm thinking Tom Cruise.

PEARL

'Come!' Lwalida pulls me towards the sink. 'Wash your face, they're ready for you!'

'But I haven't finished my food!' I try to break free, but her grip is too firm.

Zayna walks in. 'All set?'

Lwalida pinches my underarm. 'Yes she is.' I feel the tears streaming down my cheeks, wash them off with the cold water. One of the girls, probably Yasmin, starts whimpering.

'Do not be concerned, little one,' says Zayna. 'Your sister will visit often, and she'll bring you lots of wonderful presents, all the way from Madrid!'

Hearing this only makes Yasmin cry harder.

'Take her away,' orders Lwalida. 'She'll scare those poor men to death.'

I dry my face in a kitchen towel and turn to my sisters, but Zayna stands in the way. 'No time to waste, sweetheart, we can't keep the men waiting any longer.'

'I just want to say goodbye!'

Zayna comes close, and whispers into my ear, 'You continue to be disobedient if you wish, but hear this: those men out there would not hesitate to teach you and your little sisters a lesson by shearing off all your hair, and I don't mean just that dandelion patch on top of your head, in front of everyone.'

I look her straight in the eye. 'I wish you would go blind, Zanya, you old witch.'

BARBIE GIRLS

This is no country for hiding a stranger. Exposed and wide open, this land had learnt to survive by keeping itself to itself, and befriend only those invisible forces that will ask no favours of it. The land I come from, it's totally the opposite. Sticky and rich, it starts swallowing you up the minute you stop in one place for long enough. You had to keep on moving, otherwise the landscape consumed you until you became the part of it forevermore. I prefer this land. I much prefer to remain free to search for my own death, rather than being nailed to one spot, waiting for death to find me.

We sit tight next to the well, taking turns in dropping in a pail attached to it by a rope, and pouring the clear cool water over our heads. I Ching's Hexagram forty-eight, aka The Well, advises *never to leave the place your well is situated*. I think I'm okay with that.

I wake up to find Pearl praying on top of a mound she chose to sleep on last night. The sun has barely scratched the surface of the new day, and the world awaits in time-honoured silence. Why would anyone feel like they need to pray on top of such a momentous event is anyone's guess. My guess is greed.

'The best way of offering your prayers is by making sure you become one with nature at least once a day,' said Mema. 'Swim in a river, roll in the hay, climb the tree or take a walk around the garden. And don't forget to talk to it.'

'Talk to what, Mema?' I asked. 'What is *it*?'

'Everything. Droplets of rain, leaves on the tree branch, pebbles underneath your feet. Everything.'

'Is *it* like magic?'

'Exactly like magic.'

'Can I ask *it* to please buy me the Barbie I saw in the shop yesterday and my mum said no way I'm getting it for you so you can cut all her hair off. I said I promise not to do it again, but she still said no, and then she told Daddy not to buy it for me, not even as a secret.'

'Mmmm,' said Mema. 'I suppose you could try.'

So I walked around the garden, talked to ants and ladybirds, I sent telepathic massages to clouds, and climbed the quince tree outside our kitchen window at least twenty times, until one day my mum called me in, using that special tone of voice that meant either very good news, or very bad. I ran onto the porch, and as soon as I saw her and my dad, sitting side by side, smiling at me as nicely as can be, I knew it was the best news ever. They invited me to sit in the special place between them, and like a good girl I did as I was told, despite never developing the taste for spending time in a close physical proximity to either of my parents, my mother in particular.

'We've been talking,' said my dad. 'About what a good girl you've been. At school, as well as home. So we thought – what did we think, dear?'

'We thought you deserve a little treat,' said my mum. 'Everyone can do with a treat now and again; it sweetens the deal.'

So they gave me Barbie. Long blond hair, tiny waist, it came with three beautiful outfits. I stopped being one with nature right away, and a couple of days later, I cut her hair so short she ended up looking like a surprised hedgehog. Thinking back, I suspect I was plain jealous of all my Barbies, the way their hair always shone and bounced, and also the amount of sex they were having.

'Helicopter, Igor! We have to find shelter. Bloody Boss, men like him never give up.'

This is the first time I hear Pearl curse. Well – sort of curse. Am I a bad influence. Hope so.

We drink as much water as our bellies would carry – the pail is leaking all over the place, hardly worth the hassle of taking it with us. I'm still in charge of the ham, although I'm seriously toying with an idea of abandoning the pig altogether and travelling light, not to mention salt-free. The only thing that stops me is the vision of Pearl and me, crawling across a desert on our hands and knees, the sun tanning our hides into leather, and vultures flying above our heads in ever-diminishing circles. Which would be the point where ham would come in handy: vultures go for the ham, we buy ourselves the all-important Miracle Time, everyone lives. All good hopeless struggle movies contain the Miracle Time element, which is the point when the cavalry arrives and deliverance occurs despite the total and utter bleakness of the situation at hand. So the ham stays. Forward march.

'Throw it away.'

Pearl tries to grab my best friend the ham, but I won't let her.

'It will kill us,' she says. 'Too much salt. Poison.'

I reckon this is her guilt speaking. Are Muslims meant to eat pork. I think not. No wonder she's praying like, all the time. Like a proper sinner. Well she better be careful not to piss me off, otherwise I'm definitely telling Allah on her. I give her a middle finger of warning.

'Hey girl,' she says. 'You sure can argue for a dumbo!'

How dare you call me a *Dumbo*, I hate that movie. I pull her hair and run, but she still gets me by throwing a sharp object – a good size rock, as it turns out. She gets me pretty bad, I'll give her that, my head bleeds and everything, and she is oh so *bloody* sorry. So we make a pact not to resort to physical violence towards one another ever again, just in case someone gets really hurt, or we end up killing each other.

'It is enough that Boss wants us dead,' said Pearl, and for once, I agree.

Thirst is a terrible thing, far worse than hunger. I haven't peed for at least three days, and my legs are cramping so bad I would probably cry if I had any moisture left in me for tears. Meanwhile, Pearl is clutching at her chest. 'Palpitations! It is like my heart wants to jump out of my bosom.'

The way she talks is grating on me extra-hard. Who says *bosom*. Who talks this proper. What sort of person takes such trouble in pronouncing every... single... bloody... word... without... ay... fail. What sort of whore. Another thing; she's forever doing something. Moving about. Trying to sort out that bird's nest on top of her head. Chewing on her nails. Looking for the highest spot to pray on. Praying on the highest spot she could find. Talking to herself before going to sleep. In a foreign language.

The only time I find Pearl close to bearable is when I see her staring at some far away, non-place place, which is something she's been doing a lot of in the last day or two. Perhaps she's finally giving up the ghost. Try as I might, I can't see any way her death wouldn't benefit my current life situation. I mean, who am I to argue with the natural causes.

'Igor! Igor! They are here! Get up!'

I jump up so suddenly I sprain most of my major tendons, not to mention almost give myself a stroke. My eyes dart about in the darkness, scanning for Boss and his men, with their guns and their machetes a'ready, their dogs and helicopters unleashed. But there's nothing there. So the stupid girl woke me up from this great dream I was having about sex, drugs and *Dylan Dog* for no reason whatsoever.

'Look,' she says, pointing at a rock. 'I wished for them – and they appeared. It is a true miracle!'

I walk over, like a fool, but there's nothing on,

behind, around or under the fucking rock. Not a thing. Nada. Nobody. I'm about to go into a proper barking fit, but then I notice that Pearl is crying like she'll never stop, like summer rain, like a child lost.

'They were right there,' she sobs. 'The fireflies! I ask God to send us a sign, something that would tell us that everything will be okay, for me, and you, and our baby… And he did, he sent the fireflies! But now they are gone, I wanted you to witness His miracle, but they are all gone, ay. What will become of us now?'

Excuse me; what was that about *our* baby. Not my baby, you scary cuckoo girl.

'*La araña*! *Ayúdame*!'

Pearl runs into our so-called camp, screaming her head off for everyone to hear and plucking at her hair with her crazy chicken hands. I manage to catch her just as she is about to slip off the edge of a friendly neighbouring cliff. Realising how close she got to it did nothing to help cancel out the meltdown, on the contrary, it only makes it worse. I hold her down with one hand, cover her mouth with the other, all the while trying to lock her eyes together with mine, have them fix there until the dread had passed, but they remained wild, unfixable. There was nothing more I could do. Except to hold her. Which is what I do, I hold Pearl down, feeling her heartbeat, maybe even her baby's heartbeat, next to mine, and hating every moment of it.

A very long while later, once she has finally returned to being her normal annoying self, Pearl tells me what happened. It goes something like this; she was out in the campo, picking wild herbs and what not, when she walked into the biggest, stickiest *telaraña* she's ever seen. And in it lived the biggest blackest meanest-looking spider who turned bright red with rage to see his home so carelessly destroyed by a very stupid girl.

'And then he started to jump about, like upside down yo-yo. I could see poisonous spear coming out of his bottom, just as he was about to attack. But I ran fast, I ran for my life. Do you want me to show you the place? Maybe you could kill him, maybe you would enjoy killing him? Because you know what, Igor, I really think you should.'

I say nothing. Do nothing. My calf muscles are burning like hellfire. I curl up into a ball and pretend I'm dead.

'Igor? Do you see what I see? Or is this just another mirage?'

I don't exactly burst a vessel hurrying myself along to check out anything Pearl thinks she's seeing. Besides, that ship may well have already sailed, that vessel may well have already burst, because my head is throbbing so fiercely I can barely even open my eyes, let alone put them to any practical use. I imagine having the seven dwarves mining for jewels just behind my forehead. Now that's a very interesting story right there. Snow White and the Seven Dwarfs. Multifaceted. Very Germanic. But also a bit Slavic. With a touch of Welsh, too. Not my favourite, not by a long shot; nevertheless, it's a hit with the kids.

Going back to those spiders. Squeezing out their juices and bathing in them.

It's raining men. Halleluiah. Finally, I get to wash my hair.

'Why do you hate me, Mema? Is it because I'm a big girl now?'

'Fuck you, and fuck you. And as for you, well fuck you too.'

Perfume. Mercury. Paint. Kefir. Molasses. Lava. It doesn't have to be water.

This cat looks like a jaguar to me. Not a puma. Jaguar.

'Vanilla. Two scoops. And can I have it in a glass of water, please? Hold the ice.'

'Igor? Do you see what I see? Or is this just another mirage?'

I lurch to my feet and sway about the place, like a drunken toddler from Joni Mitchell's *Twisted*. Pearl catches me just as I'm about to slip off the edge of yet another friendly neighbouring cliff, although when I sort of come around moments later, there's no cliff to be seen, no chasm to fear. But there is a house on the hill in front of us. A proper house, made with red bricks and pale-yellow roof tiles, and with orange-painted columns surrounding the veranda. We encountered a couple of wooden shelters on our way – never quite managed to work out whether they were meant for sheep or shepherds – each pointlessly facing the red hot south so not exactly sheltering fuck all. But we haven't encountered a house, not until now.

'Do you see it?'

'A!' I say.

'My God, Igor! This is your second word!'

Why do women feel this need to gush about everything – especially stuff that's none of their business – I will never understand. Puts me right off talking it does.

I stare at the house. In the last five days of trekking across this land, I have realised that our pass will be more or less granted for as long as we remain small and persistent, a bit like those stinging red ants that keep congregating around Pearl, whilst kindly leaving me be. So to then grant the entire house a permission to emerge right here in its deepest midst, well it seems hardly fair. The owner must be a person of some serious influence. Like a magician, or a witch. Whoever it is, one thing is for sure; they must've had a bloody good reason to go to the trouble of building their home in the middle of such hostile nowhere.

'Careful, Igor,' says Pearl. 'This may be Boss's secret lair.'

Out of the mouth of babes.

It's a no-brainer; we either go to the house, or we die. I make Pearl sit on a rock in make-believe shadow of a scrawny bush-tree, then I set off on my highly classified mission. Or at least I try to. For some reason Pearl follows me not once but twice, and I have to escort her back to the allocated rock. The second time round, I can feel the very last strand of patience snap and fly away from me like a runaway balloon. I think she can feel it too, for she says, 'Okay, Igor. I stay.'

I climb the side of the hill leading up to the house, until I stumble upon the steps carved into stone. I take a couple at a time, suddenly feeling pretty damn good, not to mention sprightly. Guess my kidneys have received the messages from the survival centre in my brain, and are releasing the last reserves of adrenalin to help me crawl over the finishing line. Or maybe it's the sense of freedom that comes from losing my ball and chain companion that's really giving me wings.

The steps lead onto a road – proper asphalted road, none of that dirt track rubbish. There is a big iron gate to my left. To my right, the road winds itself around the bend, gradually slipping off towards the valleys. Behind me is Pearl, in front of me is another set of stone steps, scattered like baby teeth around an olive grove. I take this route, counting on it to wrap me around the house in the most sneakiest of ways.

It's very quiet out here. Eerily so. I try to remember if this is just how things roll around here, silently. I really don't know any more. Spending one 24/7 after another exposed to a noise maker couldn't have been too good for my head. I decide to sit down on the ground, and think things through.

So I go, "What if they're waiting for me, with all their weapons cocked, drawn and erected?"

Oh fuck.

I'm scared.

I'm scared, and I'm sleepy.

I open my eyes, find Pearl's crouching above me, shaking my shoulders, whispering things in the same foreign language she uses for her prayer. What have I done to deserve this. What have I ever done to you, God, personally, or otherwise.

'You fell asleep! Not good, Igor!'

She helps me to my feet, I stumble into her arms. I feel like crying, I feel sad, and I feel like crying. I feel sad for myself, mostly, but also for the world. Is this a regression into *weltschmerz*. The worst thing about *weltschmerz* is that so many people never experience it at all, not as teenagers, and not as adults. Which is also so terribly sad. What a sad, mad fuck-up this world is, what a pathetic desperate notion our lives truly are. I yelp.

'Igor? You try tell me something?' Pearl's voice pours over me like a bucket of ice cold water. I pull away from her erm *bosom*. 'Why you cry?'

And why you suddenly sound like Kunta Kinte. I motion her to follow, as she clearly won't stay put on that rock, and I just so happen to be fresh out of chains. I feel Pearl's phantom movements close behind. She makes no noise, creature of desert mirages that she is. But you can certainly feel her. I almost like this ghost-like quality she possesses. If only she never spoke.

We emerge just below the house level, to the side of the veranda. I sneak up to the wooden gates and give them a little push, just to check if they'll squeak. But they swing open without making a sound. My heart sinks. I have never come across a silent gate that someone hasn't taken trouble to oil, and usually for a good reason too. Go on, Pearl's god, help us get our supplies and leave without finding trouble. Go on,

Pearl's god, and I'll never call her a stupid puta, ever again.

We enter the veranda. The vines have set into a thick canopy above our heads, creating the best shade this side of Mema's walled garden. I wait for my eyes to adjust.

'Visitors! How wonderful! Charlotte, dear, bring two more glasses – we have guests!'

ART OF WAR

Before I know it, I'm shaking a badly gnarled hand presented to me by a tall old lady who I swear materialised in front of us from nowhere. It feels younger than it looks. The hand, I mean. Hands can be awkward. Once your hands grow old, that's it. No amount of plastic surgery will rejuvenate them. All you can do is wear gloves. And how do I know this? Because I once watched this film called *Fedora*, which had the best hand-twist in the history of cinema.

Other than her hands, the old lady looks pretty neat – immaculate black bob, discreetly applied make-up, spotless khaki linen shirtdress, and so on. Proper dame, she reminds me of one of those plucky female explorers who trudged through the deepest darkest Africa at the turn of the century. People like her wouldn't wear gloves for anybody. I know I've only just met her, but I bet she wouldn't give a fuck about what other people thought of her witchy old fingers.

'I'm Ivy,' she says. There's a pause. Quite a long one. Ivy holds my gaze with a twinkle in her eye. 'Oops, I blinked, you win!' She turns to Pearl. I suddenly feel abandoned. 'And who's the little one? What a magnificent mane, like a desert lioness!'

'Mother, darling!' Another, younger woman appears on the veranda. 'Lionesses don't have manes – lions do!' She slams down a tray on a large rectangular table, causing Pearl to jump out of her scaredy-cat skin. 'Sorry, ladies – it slipped.'

She then collapses into a chair and starts fiddling with her sunglasses. Off they go, back on again, until she eventually settles on wearing them on the top of her head.

I'm thinking, "This lady is pissed!" I mean *really* pissed, like she went for a drink one balmy summer eve circa 1974 and had never put it down since. I like her already, in the same way I liked Bella the first time I saw her. She's not as lovely as Bella was, but is still sort of pretty, especially for an old woman. Like I said, not as old as Ivy, who's absolutely ancient. This one may be something like forty, with short, coppery hair, and freckles sprayed all over her nose and cheeks. How cute. I used to long to look cute, sport freckles and ponytails, play nicely in a sandpit with other little girls. Another childhood dream that bit the dust big time. The lady looks at me with eyes the colour of early June cornflowers, shame about the dark circles underneath. Kidneys. Mema used to pound her middle back every evening, so she wouldn't wake up with dark circles under her eyes. 'You must make sure your kidneys stay alert, because if they work, everything else works, and you wake up feeling and looking as fresh as a daisy!'

'I know that, silly!' Ivy lets out a regal cackle. 'Come and meet our guests – I'm yet to learn their names.'

'My name is Pearl, ma'am. And this is Igor.'

Ma'am? You can take the girl out of the service, but you can't take the service out of the girl.

'Oh, please, call me Ivy. And this is my daughter, Charlotte.'

Charlotte waves. 'Drink?'

It would be rude to wait to be asked twice. I ignore the jar of freshly made lemonade and even the bourbon, and go straight for the old fashioned soda syphon. The first attempt to fill my glass isn't a great success, with soda spraying all over the place, least of all into a glass. But I get the knack the second time around, and the third, and I'm just about to fill my glass for the fourth time when a random hand grabs my wrist. I look up, a soft growl rumbling from deep within my throat.

'How about you slow down a bit, eh love?' Charlotte lets go and gently pries the glass away. 'Take it easy. Have a bourbon.'

'How precious!' says Ivy. 'Where's my camera? I want to make a documentary. Charlotte, dear, bring me my equipment!'

Charlotte doesn't move an inch, except to pour a finger of a dark amber liquid into a glass, and hand it over to me. I down it in one. She refills it. I do the same. And so it goes, in silence, for three more quick fire rounds. I'm aware of Pearl, lurking somewhere in the background, which is where I'd prefer her to stay. Ivy is wandering around the table, talking to her outstretched hand, 'Yes little ladybird, you may. No, it is not an inconvenience. Not at all. You're most welcome. We appreciate your custom.'

The ghost of a familiar scent glides onto the veranda. I know it and I simply *adore* it, as the ladies would no doubt have it. I can only describe the scent as a mellower version of lily of the valley, with a hint of day old snow sprinkled on top. I must inform Charlotte. She is such a generous host, I need to give her something in return. Give her this fragrance. Right now, she may be too pissed to distinguish her olfactory perception from her ass, but unless I instruct her, she may never learn about the magical scent living on her very doorstep.

So I stand on a chair and start instructing.

Charlotte gazes up at me in wonder. 'What is she doing?'

'I am not sure, ma'am.' Pearl joins the front row. 'She might be reciting a poem. Her, um, father was very fond of poetry.'

'Mmmm-hmm? B! B! ZB!' I boom. 'Shhhmmmm-akhhhhhhhh-mmmm. D-d-d-d-d-d!'

Charlotte claps. 'Wonderful stuff! Very experimental.'

'Superb, dear Igor!' says Ivy. 'Bravo!'

Mema always said I would make a good actress.

I open my eyes and have no idea:

a) who I am,

b) where I am, and

c) if I'm even supposed to know the answers to questions a) and b).

But the room is dark, my body doesn't hurt, I'm all alone, gods must be merciful for a change, is all I need to know, over and out.

The next time I open my eyes, I am not so lucky.

'Who are you?' I raise myself onto my elbows, feeling as weak as a kitten that went and drowned in a bottle of bourbon. Charlotte is leaning against the wall, smoking a cigarette, staring at me across the room with a nasty glint in her eye. 'Why did you come here?'

I shut my eyes in hope she'll go away.

'I know you're awake. No use pretending.' I feel the side of the bed depress, as she sits on it. Awkward. I decide it's time to get up and maybe put on some clothes. Off I pop then. 'Hey! Where do you think you're going?'

I force myself into a semblance of composure. Calmly, slowly and orderly, I let my hand slip off the door handle, and turn around to face her. I'm not too good at playing polite and other such barbaric games, but Pearl and I need supplies, and a medium-size donkey to lug our stuff, if they happen to have one going spare. This means we need Charlotte. What we don't need is her running to Boss, or the police, or god forbid both.

I read it somewhere that the act of smiling activated the happiness motherboard of our brains, so I offer Charlotte one of my bestest brightest smiles. A happy person is a generous person. Or do I mean drunk. I once gave away my own bra to this random girl I was sharing a bottle of vodka with, I was that pissed. Or was I just happy. And is there even a difference.

'What are you doing?' Charlotte asks. 'Don't you dare crap yourself, do you hear me?'

I stop smiling.

On second thoughts, who needs a favour from this drunken bitch, this *borracha*? Not me is for sure. I slam the door on my way out, and go in search of Ivy.

'Igor! At last! You slept for three days, girl, I was getting worried about you!'

I find Pearl pottering around the kitchen like she owned it. She's wearing somebody's purple dress with a yellow overall, and proper whistling while she works. The grey shadow of death has moved on for the time being, leaving her looking young(ish) and fresh again. For a moment there I find myself considering whether we should kill Ivy and Charlotte and stay here assuming their lives and identities, but try as I might – which is to say, not very hard – I can't really see us pulling it off.

'You must be hungry, girl! I make you some nice French toast, and coffee, how about it?'

I almost smile, then think better of it.

'What was that? Was that a smile? Go on, Igor, you look pretty when you smile.'

I look out of the window so she can't see me blush. And also because I'm about to cry, *again*.

Sadness blows, no doubt about that. It gives you an itch you cannot scratch, a wound that refuses to heal, a black dog that won't leave you alone. But there is a cure, and I should know, because I bloody well invented it:

a) never mention to anyone you're feeling sad. Make sure your sadness is your best protected secret. If you were the world's politics, your sadness would be the Pentagon;

b) never think about it. Develop a strategy, like banging your head against the wall every time a sad thought enters your mind. Your body will quickly learn to disassociate from whatever it is that's causing it worse pain, and

c) keep on practising the points a) and b) until the very memory of sadness completely disappears. You will still *know* that there is sadness in your life, but you will forget what it actually feels like. At this stage, it's best to leave well alone: under no circumstances you are to start opening up to people, or indulging in reflection on any subject that involves your inner world. Remember, sadness is always there, waiting for a chance to spark back into your life – don't take no risks, okay.

d) NB – what I'm talking about here is your personal sadness, the so-called pain within. You are still allowed to feel sad for ET not making it home, or a baby antelope being mauled to death by a bunch of hyenas (unless of course you're one of those people who find this sort of thing amusing). Depersonalised sadness is absolutely fine, because it means fuck all. Just make doubly sure you never *ever* start identifying with the plight of others: this is a slippery slope, so keep it in, keep it at bay, keep it detached. Be a winner, baby.

Ivy waltzes up to the window frame – I mean literally waltzes, as in waltzing around the veranda all by her lonesome – then fades out of view again.

'These women are kind,' says Pearl. 'But funny. Rich ladies, they are all little crazy.'

I climb out of the window and land onto the

veranda. Ivy doesn't notice me, lost in a whirl of her own making. 'And one and two and six and seven-eight! And two and six and five and thirty-four!'

Mema used to be a ballerina when she was young. Her dream was to dance for the Bolshoi, but that never happened.

'I developed too much love for life to become a top ballerina. I ate too much bread and kissed too many boys. Besides, the Bolshoi, it's full of hot air, and Russians. I would've never fitted in.'

Mema tried to teach me ballet, but I was too impatient.

'You are too much of a free spirit to be a ballerina,' she declared, after I danced my way through two or three lessons like a stick on sticks. 'I shall be teaching your sister from now on.'

I knew this was a good thing. Not for me, prancing around in a tutu. But my sister, she loved it.

'You're useless at dancing,' she said. 'I saw you, you couldn't even manage a plié.'

'Fuck off,' I said. 'Can't you see I'm reading?'

Just then, Ivy waltzes by and grabs hold of my hand, and the next thing I know I'm being dragged right out my childhood reverie, and across the tiles by the strange old lady with a dance habit.

'And a top of the morn to you, young man,' she says. 'Did Frank see you sneak in?'

I shake my head. No wonder she didn't find it curious I go under a boy's name. She thinks I *am* a boy. Or worse – a man.

'Isn't this fun?' she asks. 'Let's step it up a notch!'

160

Round and round we go, Ivy and me, faster and faster, round and round we twirl, until I feel like I'm about to be sick and have to pull out, and quick.

'Have I exhausted you, my love?'

I take an emergency time-out on the bench underneath the kitchen window, feeling a cool breeze stroking the back of my neck. I do some shallow yoga breathing through my mouth, until I feel even more dizzy. Pearl pops her head out of the window. 'Oh Igor, that was so funny! You and Ivy, dancing like lovers. Here is some French toast for you, with cinnamon and strawberries, just as you like it.'

She puts the plate on the table and I throw up all over it.

I open my eyes, take one hundred and fifty-five, but this time I know exactly what to do. It's time to get the fuck out of here, kick some dust, hit the road, burn some serious rubber. I jump out of bed, discover that someone's taken away my clothes, probably to wash, probably that idiot Pearl, never happy unless she's doing some sort of slave labour. There is a dress hanging off the doorframe, presumably left out for me to wear. A polka dot halter dress. God I'm so angry right now.

I march into the kitchen, where I find all three of them, chatting about something Pearl's cooked – and I'm not even lying.

'Igor! You are up!' Pearl claps her hands. 'Are you hungry?'

'Igor! Don't you look pretty!' Charlotte's voice is back to its original mellow, welcoming even. What's up with that. Where's the scary Gestapo woman who sat on my bed demanding some answers, *und schnell*. 'Drink?'

She pours a generous splash of vodka into a couple of glasses, pushes one over to me. The fact that at this point Ivy starts talking to herself and wringing her hands doesn't escape the all-seeing eye of my superhero perception. Seems to me the old bird doesn't like the slightly less old bird drinking. But I do. I like dealing with Mrs Hyde, she's far more malleable than the other version of Charlotte. Prost. I raise my glass, and she meets me half way. I don't drink mine, I pour it out of the window. Drinking and doing shit don't make a great mix. I need a sober head, not to mention body, for whatever's coming next.

'Charlotte,' says Ivy. 'I thought you said you were on a diet.'

'Mother! Are you saying I'm fat?'

'Not fat, darling. Just a bit puffy.'

'Oh Mother, you are funny,' says Charlotte. 'We just got ourselves a cook, and you want me to stop eating.'

Cook, what cook.

'It's not so much about what you *eat*, dear–'

I slam the glass against the marble surface. Everyone jumps, even me. 'In the land of the blind, the one-eyed man is king,' Mema used to say on those rare occasions when she watched the evening news. Well I reckon it's about time for this king, i.e. me, to lead the blind, i.e. Pearl, out of here, then hand her over to the first Interpol-looking person we come across.

'What's up with Igor?' asks Charlotte. 'She looks cross.'

'That boy is a marvellous dancer, you know,' says Ivy. 'But don't tell Fred.'

I march into the storeroom, with Pearl pussyfooting in my wake. 'Igor? What are you doing?' I start gathering supplies for the journey ahead – a large bottle of water, a couple of boxes of crackers, half a dozen tins of tuna fish, one dry-cured salami, two packs of mints and a dried fig wheel. I pop everything into an old wicker basket, with two handy wide leather strips attached to its side, and hey presto, we're good to go. I place the basket on my back, take Pearl's hand and head towards the door.

'Oh my,' says Charlotte. 'I think Igor's trying to steal our cook.'

'Let go!' Pearl pulls away. 'I stay here!'

I throw the basket on the floor, and grab hold of her shoulders. She struggles. 'Let go of me, girl!'

I can be incredibly strong, but only under what you'd call extreme conditions. Bella's death was one, it brought on the tunnel vision; all I could see were these two little pins of light somewhere way down the line, too far away to make a difference to my life, or anyone else's for that matter. The dogs, the smiling old man. There was no escape. No hope. The old man, I saw he wasn't going to budge, wasn't going to let us go, and for a moment I was almost fine with that. Then suddenly, time slowed right down, and it stretched, and I could see the specks of dust dancing around the rays of orange sun, and a could see a small muscle twitch just below the left corner of his crooked mouth, and I could see a fly, about to land on my knee, before changing its mind and disappearing off into the back of the truck. But the moment I picked up that machete, the time sped up again, took me and everyone else with it.

Well. Whatever the mystery ingredient is, this situation seems to be lacking it. I'm not feeling especially strong, quite the opposite. Just goes to show that you cannot rely on your inner crazy to get you out of a pickle. Crazy's unpredictable, it comes on when it wants to, as for the rest of the time, you're on your own.

So I let go of Pearl, she flies back into the kitchen unit and bashes her head against the open cupboard door. 'Ahhh,' she goes, and slips down to the floor.

'My goodness!' Ivy runs towards Pearl, then changes her mind and runs over to the wide open window. 'Help, help! Somebody! Call a doctor!'

'No need for a doctor, Mama.' Charlotte pours herself another drink, polishes it off, then pours another and walks over to me. 'We'll take care of this.' She hands me the drink. 'Won't we, Igor?'

DON'T FENCE ME IN

So now no one's speaking to me. I am being shunned by the entire local population, and the memories of my schooldays flood back in. No one does shunning better than a pack of ten-year-old dogs – I meant girls.

'Why don't they like me, Mema?'

'Because you're different,' said Mema. 'They are afraid of you.'

'Why can't I be more like them?'

'You just can't. You are cut from a different cloth, there's nothing you can do about that. But one day you'll be glad you were not like them.'

'Really, Mema?'

'Oh yes.'

'Okay then. Because I only pretend to want to be like them. I don't. What I really want is line them up in front of a wall and burn them to cinders with my flamethrower. Like Nazis did with partisans, except I'd be a partisan commander hero and they'd be the Nazi pigs.'

'Cruelty doesn't become you,' said Mema. 'Would you like another piece of apple pie?'

I'm sitting in the corner of the veranda, all by my lonesome, watching the three witches gathered around the table, whispering about me no doubt. I feel like a child, made to sit with other invisible children at a spazzy little table while the adults dined at the big table in the middle of the room.

'Tell them, Mema,' I said. 'Tell them I'm not little.'

'It's not about being little,' said my fat auntie Alda. 'It's about being a kid.'

I ignored the stupid old whale. 'Mema. Tell them.'

'This girl here,' Mema said. 'Is not little.'

'What does she want now?' My mum had a thing about special favours and privileges. 'Why must you always demand a special treatment?'

'I'm not,' I said. 'Tell her, Mema.'

'You need to learn to speak for yourself,' my mum said. 'Otherwise you'll never get what you want.'

'Can I sit at the grown-up table?' I asked.

'Don't be so silly,' said my mum. 'Children sit at the children's table. Stop fussing, we're trying to eat.'

'God save us from precocious children,' said Aunt Alda. 'They make our soup go cold.'

'Precisely!' said Mum. 'Go and sit in your place, now!'

I looked at Mema, feeling that all was lost. Except that maybe it wasn't. Because Mema stood up, removed the napkin from her lap and placed it onto her plate. She was a tall woman, my Mema, and when a woman like her stood up, the whole room couldn't help but shut the fuck up.

'If a child speaks and we refuse to listen, then why have we brought it into this world in the first place?

'To look after us when we get old and decrepit,' says Aunt Alda. 'Why else?'

One or two people laughed, but even I could tell their hearts weren't in it.

'That, Alda, is the saddest thing I have ever heard,' said Mema. 'If we deny the new life its authentic voice, if we smother it from the very start, then what hope is there left for the rest of us?'

'None whatsoever,' said Uncle Mirko, who was famous for his greedy gut and also for being my sister's short-straw godfather. 'The girl may sit with us. Let's eat.'

'Igor?' Charlotte calls out. 'Come over here, please, we need to have a word.'

So I'm being summoned am I. Right now, I can see very little difference between these women and Boss. The fact they don't sex-traffic girls or kill anyone who steps out of line doesn't make them any less annoying. Where's my flamethrower when I need it the most.

I walk over, like some pitiful p-word: a puppy or a pauper or a puppet on a string, painfully aware I could simply turn around and walk the other way. Except I can't. And don't. Has my life come to this.

'Go on, love,' says Charlotte. 'We won't bite.'

Did she just call me love? If she's not careful, Charlotte may just take the much sought after title of my arch-nemesis, currently held by the blissfully unsuspecting Pearl. Drunken Charlotte is okay, all mellow and devil may care. Sober, she turns into dust. I sit on the bench, but refuse to make eyes with anyone. They may as well realise I'm here under duress and totally against my own far superior judgment.

'We want you to stay here, with us,' says Charlotte. 'As in, live here. Pearl told us the whole story, about Boss, and the baby, and about you killing that old man.'

I lose my cool there for a moment, shoot Pearl a look of pure hatred.

'No use looking at her like that,' says Charlotte. 'She did the right thing. At least now we all know where we stand, and can prepare ourselves accordingly.'

'Preparing French beans can be tricky,' says Ivy. 'First you must remove all the string. As a matter of fact, I don't think I like them, please make sure they're off the menu.'

'Yes, ma'am,' says Pearl. 'Consider it done.'

'Good girl,' says Ivy. 'We eat our lunch at high noon in this country. Like in that movie, er… Charlotte dear, what was the title of that movie that rhymes with lunch?'

'*High Noon*?' says Charlotte.

'Yes, that one,' says Ivy. 'You always were a good guesser! Gary Cooper, now he was what you'd call a real man! But my favourite was Rock Hudson, oh I adored him so!' She leans in towards me, whispers, 'He turned out to be a queer, you know.'

A sanctuary is the place you run to when chased by a hostile element. It is also a title of a book by William Faulkner, about a nasty thing happening to a young girl. The perpetrator then stashes her away at this horrible place where things steadily progress from bad to plain evil, until the darkness swallows them all. Truth be told, I've forgotten the actual ending, my point being that Charlotte and Ivy's house feels like Faulkner type of a sanctuary to me, which is to say, not very sanctuarious. All it will take is a knock on the door, and that'll be the end of all of us chickens cooped up in here, clucking away like there's no tomorrow, wasting time.

Tomorrow is coming.

Boss is coming.

For Pearl and me, especially me.

I wonder how Princess is doing. Whether she misses me at all.

'Why are you staring at me still?' Pearl is making ham and pea soup. Earlier, she made me shell the peas, a whole mountain of slippery green fuckers. I had to sit there for ages, breaking into one little pod after another, and eating quite a few, until they gave me shits. 'And have you washed your hands, eh?'

My stomach hurts. I need a beer. It's not logical, but then again logic never made much sense in my life. I grab a bottle from the fridge, notice we're running alarmingly low. Other, less important, things, too, like for example bread and milk and maybe butter. Still not sure if I like butter, or really hate it. I reckon that if I continue spreading it on everything I eat, it'll come to me in the end.

Supplies. How does that happen around here.

I open and close the fridge door until I get Pearl to look. 'What you want now?'

I point at the empty shelves, turn my palms up and shrug my shoulders.

'You need toilet again? Why do you have to tell

me, girl? Just go, before you have an accident.'

Stupid is what stupid sees.

I shake my head, stomp my foot and point inside the fridge. Then, with my best mime expression, I indicate there's fuck all left to eat, all the beer's gone and what I'd like to know is what happens when we run out completely, particularly with regards to beer.

'You are behaving like child,' says Pearl. 'So I am going to treat you like child and ask that you go out and play until I call you in for dinner.'

'She wants more beer.' Charlotte's propping up the door, just about. 'As do I, but for purely medicinal purposes.' She holds up her hands, which tremble so bad it looks like she's playing invisible drums. 'The bourbon appears to be having a detrimental effect upon my central nervous system of late. Bloody nuisance, if you ask me.' She shoves her hands into large patch pockets of her apron. 'Hey-ho. It'll be out of my system in a couple of days, then I'll be as good as new. Trouble is, I must have the beer to help me land. The last time I went cold turkey I ended up fitting so bad I almost bit off my own tongue. Scared poor mother half to death.' She gives Pearl a glassy stare. 'So someone needs to go down to the village – someone who's not me.'

Pearl gapes. She does this a lot. If she likes something, she gapes. If she doesn't like something, she also gapes. She gapes when she can't comprehend a situation, and she does it when she's scared. The woman is a gaper. Oh Jett, oh Jett, oh Jett. Hope one day he'll appreciate my sacrifice and show his gratitude in the most incredible of ways. Can't think of anything right now, except a newspaper cone filled with charred sweet chestnuts. And a crate of beer.

Back to so-called reality, well if Charlotte can't drive on account of her blossoming state of delirium tremens, then who the hell can. Ivy strolls in, does a little twirl in the middle of the kitchen, then waltzes off back onto the veranda. I point after her. Charlotte laughs. Not her usual, roaring fire laugh which I find strangely reassuring; this time she sounds more like a freshly extinguished pile of ashes.

'*Mother*? Are you fucking with me, love? My mother is the woman who isn't here, you understand?' Charlotte lights a cigarette, has some trouble holding her hands still enough to marry the lighter to the tip. 'Truth be told, she would probably benefit from getting some professional help. But if I take her back to the old country, they'll just stick her into some institution. She has other children beside me, see. The good ones, decent, pillars of community. Bella and Ludovick. Feels strange to say their names, it's been so long. And all Bella and Ludovick care about is mother's money. I may be a drunk, but those two have no sense of honour to speak of. They want us dead, you know.'

'Oh dear!' says Pearl. 'Gasp!'

She doesn't actually say *gasp*, but that's what I hear alright. Pearl is not only a gaper but a gasper, and at the risk of sounding like a broken record, I can't wait for the day Jett's people take her off my hands and my mind already. The more I say this, the more chance of it actually happening, is what I'm counting on.

'It's true,' says Charlotte. 'They want Mum and me out of the way, so they can do as they please with what's left of the estate. Why would anyone choose to live in this godforsaken corner of the world, unless they were hiding from death?'

My sentiment exactly.

'So you see, Pearl, it's up to you now,' says Charlotte. 'To save the day.'

Pearl gasps then gapes, the silly Sahara plant.

'You do drive, yes?'

Pearl shakes her head. 'No, Miss, please do not ask, anything but go out.'

'Why on earth not?' Charlotte's been scratching the same spot on her left arm for the last two days. Is she a heroin addict now. And how come Charlotte gets heroin and I don't. 'Why can't you go out? Is it agoraphobia?'

'I think you may be right, Miss,' says Pearl. 'As you know, those men liked to slip the condom off just before, you know'

'Slip you one?' Charlotte chortles. 'I always wondered how one gets agoraphobia. And now I know.'

'Miss Charlotte,' says Pearl. 'Do you think – do you think I could die from it?'

I can't hold it in any longer, I laugh so hard I have to bend over and hold my sides to stop them from splitting.

'The sound of a mute laughing,' says Charlotte. 'I shall never sleep again.'

Well that was most definitely uncalled for.

The Jeep is old and covered in spiders' webs of the stickiest sort. There is an abandoned nest at the back seat, a couple of broken eggshells gathering dust. Hopefully it was a bird that hatched out of it, and not a serpent. Or a dragon. Wouldn't want a dragon offspring messing up my hair whilst I'm driving around the precipitous terrain that stands in between me and my beer.

I stick the key into the engine and turn. Nothing. Again. Nothing. I look at Charlotte, who's very visibly using the barn wall as her only means of support, shaking like the tail of the rattlesnake I pray hasn't crawled out of that eggshell at the back. I turn again, the engine coughs, once, twice – and then it starts to purr. Like a proper tomcat, with his belly full of cream. I'm so happy I could scream, but don't want to provoke any more of the vitriolic and quite frankly racist remarks about mutes from Charlotte, so I keep it nice and schtum. Besides, I can scream as much as I like as loudly as I like on my way to the village. This is going to be the best supplies mission like, ever.

'Not so fast,' says Charlotte. 'Pearl, have you got the stuff I asked for?'

'Yes, ma'am. I left it on that bench over there.'

Charlotte beckons me to follow her. Oh fuck what now. The moment I slip off the seat, Ivy slips her bony ass into it. I go back and grab the keys, but she doesn't care about that, she's already spinning the wheel all over town, driving some place fine and dandy no doubt; up, up and away, off goes Ivy into the Never Never Land and beyond.

'Look at Ivy,' says Pearl. 'She is pretending to be a driver.'

I push Pearl out of my way, even though and strictly speaking she wasn't actually in my way to start off with, just to teach a lesson on pointing the obvious.

'Ouch,' she goes. 'Watch how you go!'

'Igor, darling, would you mind taking off your top, please?' Her words read benevolent enough, but Charlotte's voice is cracking up and loosing frequency all over the joint, like an old radio that's about to expire for once and for all. I shake my head and fold my arms across my chest. No means no. Back off, you pervy witch. Charlotte sighs, which sounds to me a lot like a sob. 'Igor. Darling. If you go to the village as you are, you will get caught. That Boss of yours, bet he has his eyes and ears all over the place by now. The only way you may stand a chance of making it is if you go in disguise. Trust me, okay, I used to be a wardrobe and make-up girl with the National Theatre, or at least I think I was. In any case, I know what I'm doing.'

I shake my head, but slower this time. In case she missed the no bit.

'What is it with you, eh?' Charlotte tries to light a cigarette, but her fingers twitch and snap it in half. 'Why can't you just do what you're told? You're supposed to be a whore, aren't whores supposed to do what they're bloody told?'

I know Charlotte's being out of line, but I don't feel it. All I feel is kind of sorry for her. To hell with it. To hell with it all. I strip off my top and stand in the sunshine pouring in through the wide open door. She looks me in the eye, starts crying. Must be touched by my beautifulness. I sort of admire Charlotte for going through all this shit instead of reaching into the drink cabinet and downing a bottle of vodka. Perhaps there is strength to be found in every kind of weakness. Is this something Mema told me, or am I turning into a guru.

Gently, almost shyly, Charlotte starts wrapping a strip of gauze around my chest, binding my breasts into a flat surface worthy of any boy. Once it's done, she hands me a white vest made from thick ribbed cotton, a pair of old jeans and a chequered short-sleeved shirt.

'And the last but not least…' She tops it all off by placing a knackered New York Yankees baseball hat on top of my head. I stare at my reflection in a large piece of a dim mirror wedged in between the wall and a rusty wheelbarrow, and I'm fucked if I can see any difference. But Charlotte seems pleased. Even Pearl smiles at me in an approving sort of way, not that anyone's asked for her participation.

'Just one more thing…' Charlotte runs her hand over the back of an ancient lawnmower, then brushes her fingers across my face and bare arms. 'Perfect!'

'And who's this handsome fellow?' Ivy's best wolf-whistle attempt ends up with her false teeth shooting right out of her mouth, which is the best party trick I saw for a long time. 'Oh? What was that? A shooting star? How lovely.'

After a few minutes of faffing about the cockpit floor, I retrieve the runaway gnashers and return them to their baffled host. Then I'm out of there, I'm free, I'm on the road again, and for that moment there at least I'm as happy as can be.

DEAD GIRL'S GHOST

I jump out of the Jeep and throw up by the side of the road, before finding a clean patch of grass to collapse onto, feeling squeezed out and basically like I was about to die. A glimpse of freedom, and I'm already writhing on the floor. What am I supposed to do, give up on the whole idea, embrace the life of a slave, a battery chicken and a tethered falcon, wait for my master to fuck me, slay me, fly me, huh, is that my karma for this stupid so-called lifetime. You want freedom, eh little Igor? You can't handle the freedom. You stupid cunt. You moron. You fucking dirty skunky waste of space.

On the positive side, they say that once you lose the last ounce of self-respect, you have nothing else left to lose. So this is what's gonna happen here: I will get back into that Jeep, and drive on into that village. I'll fill up on petrol and buy a ten-pack Marlboro Red. And some churros if they got any. And a box of matches. Okay – and a bottle of beer. A large one. But only one. Then I'll just drive on. And on. I'll never look back, except to check my rear-view mirrors. I'll drive until I run out of petrol and cash, and then I'll hitchhike the rest of the way. Or maybe I'll just walk

– see how I feel nearer the time – until I get myself into the nearest city, where I will insist on speaking only to the most important police official. No, not the police. I need an international guy, like Jett. But way higher up the tree. A powerful guy, who would not succumb to political pressure to keep the country's slate appear nice and clean by, say, vanishing some innocent yet super courageous informer into the blackest, bleakest hole this side of the edge of the universe.

I mean, how do you actually get to traffic one bunch of women after another across the continent without anyone giving a shit, let alone trying to stop it. I sort of get how stuff like heroin gets smuggled in and out, but you can hardly swallow a bag of whores and shit them out on the other side of the border. How does Boss do it, when people like my dad could barely smuggle a couple of Trappist cheeses on the way back from our Hungary spa holiday.

'You only bought one, right?' He kept asking my mother as we queued at the Hungarian border. I was a proper happy girl back then, having just spent two weeks at the liveliest, funnest spa town in the world, seducing every Czech boy who was too slow to get out of my path in time to save his heart. 'Remember, we are not allowed to take more than one kilogram of hard cheese across the border.'

'That's a shame,' my mum said. 'Because there are four two kilogram blocks of cheese in the icebox under the girls' seat, plus ten pairs of those lovely paprika sausages from the Harkány butcher you played chess with every evening.'

'Jesus!' My dad started up the engine. 'We must get out of this line, now!'

'Have you gone mad?' My mum said. 'Do you want the entire Hungarian army after us?'

'But we are smuggling their *goods*!' My dada wiped his sweaty brow with a handkerchief. 'Which makes us the *smugglers*! And in this country smugglers go to jail. Have I not told you *not* to buy food, have I not warned you what will happen to us if you do?'

'You said a lot of things,' my mum said. 'Just relax, show the man your passport, and please stop panicking, you silly man!'

My sister couldn't take the tension, and burst into tears. Naturally, I then slapped her, she screamed, and I threw her doll out of the window, just to teach her a lesson.

'What the–'

My dad was just about to whack both of our legs, I knew he was so I pulled mine out of his reach, when a young border control officer walked up to our VW beetle, carrying my sister's doll – and handing it back to me, because I was the prettier and the more interesting one. He smiled, and I fell in love with him there and then. I used to fall in love all the time, I did. Spent all my loving then, I suspect. These days, when I say I love Jett or whoever, I'm only fucking around. It's not for real. Then, it was pure, it was the real flames of love licking me up, burning me down, twisting my knickers all over town.

'Where baby passport?' he asked, pigeon-style cute.

'What?' my dad went. 'Baby, I mean, doll – oh! She needs a passport?' He turned to my mum. 'Dolly needs a passport, honey, I told you to make sure everyone had all the necessary papers.'

We all laughed, even my spastic sister. The nice border control guy then waved us through, letting us jump a million kilometres worth of line.

'Call yourself a professor,' said Mum. 'Can't even smuggle a piece of cheese across a friendly border.'

I feel a little better now. And a little worse, for all the thinking I just did. This always happens when alcohol starts to leave my body, the brain kicks in with a vengeance, probably to show me that no matter how many of its cells I kill, it is still the boss of me. Well fuck off brain. You wait till I get me a beer.

I climb back into the Jeep, and get back on the road. Down and down it goes, spiralling along the edge of the mountain. I see the village, at the bottom, and my heart yelps with excitement. And also dread. Why must there always be dread. I flip open the sunshade, glance inside a cracked mirror. I look pale, as Mema would say. 'You look so pale, my girl. Strip down to your knickers and go sit in the sun, let the rays wash off the ghastly pallor unbecoming of a live spark such is yourself.' One thing's for sure – I haven't looked like my live spark self for years. And just like that, my eyes fill up with tears. Of anger, of course. Not a sentimental soul, mine. But I do feel angry a lot. Like for example, I'm really pissed off I never had a chance to wear my brand new dress, the one that burnt down together with my almost but not quite forgotten home. I left it hanging on the wardrobe door, waiting for me to break it in once the time was supremely right. I can see it now: pale grey linen, long and habit-like, with a white collar and neat vertical pleats running along both front and back. My perfectionist seamstress had me over for fitting at least half a dozen times, and it really was the best fit ever. But I never got to wear it. And now I never will. This is the anger worth feeling, the stolen dress anger. I believe this is the very anger that took away my voice.

I park the Jeep just outside the village, underneath a gnarly fig tree. A couple of scruffy old dogs appear from the nearby shed, but keep their distance. I feel their unblinking eyes on me as I walk around in my manly swagger. 'Whatever you do, do not slouch,' said Charlotte. 'Remember, you no longer have any breasts to hide from the world, so walk straight. I said *straight*. Not figure eight. Go on, like you mean it.'

The thing is, I don't mean it. Part of me is sick of pretending to be someone I'm not. Part of me craves a showdown. In one of Boss's books, not sure if it was Sidney Sheldon or Harold Robbins, a group of banditos are pillaging and raping all over town, before finally getting caught. The person in charge of the rival gang lines them up, then gives his pistol to a little girl, tells her to aim for their dicks. Banditos are laughing, thinking no way she's going to do it. Except she does, she shoots their dicks clean off, one by one, until they're all thrashing about the blood-soaked ground, not only in deep agony, but also realisation they no longer have the one thing that qualified them as real men. That's the type of a showdown I fancy. And if the whole situation were to turn against me, I think I'd be safe in the knowledge that Boss would never let me survive whatever punishment he decided to inflict upon me, so it's a win-win, result wise, no matter what.

'What a load of bullshit,' says the part of me that just wants to live happily ever after. I'm not too proud of this part of me, and blame Mema for keeping it alive. 'You are a child of gentle winds and lucky stars,' she once told me, and once is all it took. 'Make sure you do what comes naturally to you, then you will know the state of beauty and harmony forevermore.' The way I see it, she basically fucking promised that I was destined to be okay, more than okay – that I was destined to be happy and free. So what's up with the war, and whores, and the war of whores following me around like a nasty case of ass flies.

Right. Enough bullshit already. This my chance to leave it all behind. And you know what, I'm not even going to bother with Interpol. Fuck that. Pearl and Charlotte and Ivy are going to be fine. Especially Ivy, because she's lost most of her marbles and can no longer tell if things are turning good or bad. It's all good now in Ivy's world. As for Charlotte, she's going to be okay as long as she continues to drink. I wouldn't recommend sobriety to her. Too harsh, plus it's a bit too late to start changing now, at her ripe old age of forty-something would be my guess. Pearl, well the best thing for her to do is to drop the infant, I mean – have a baby, then leave Ivy and Charlotte to take care of it and either go back to whoring, or return to her desert home, get a husband, start all over. Bet she could get any husband she likes, once she's shown him all the bedroom tricks she had picked up along the way. I think I got it sussed, and I sort of wish I could write down a few instructions and send it to them in a letter, but I don't have the address. Maybe they'll figure it out anyway. My gut feeling tells me Boss will not bother them there, and besides, Charlotte has a shotgun so it's not like they have absolutely no defence. I mean, it's not my job to be anyone's protector. I have done my share of major good deeds by looking after Pearl for as long as I have, and it's been way too long, if you ask me. The last thing I want is to create attachments and dependency, which by the way is an exclusively human trait. Every other animal encourages their young to fend for themselves, their old and decrepit curl up and die in a polite fashion, and their stupids roam around quite freely, until they fall off a cliff or get stuck in a washing machine and drown.

To say this village is sleepy would be like calling a comatose person a circus acrobat. The streets are empty, the white-washed houses white and silent, with shutters bolted tight against the sun. I feel like I've entered a ghost movie set. Not too fond of ghosts, me, mainly because there is no rhyme or reason to them, they come and go as they please, silent and invisible. No breath, no thump, no presence. Until they get you. I don't know how they get you, on account of being non-corporeal and all, maybe they simply drive you mad until you chop off your own head, or get stuck in a washing machine and drown.

Yikes.

Compared to ghosts, Boss and his pervy crew sure seem like a flock of squabbling parrots. It's easy to get totally paranoid when you're on the run, thinking everyone and everything is out to get you. But seriously, I bet they've moved on like ages ago, or moved on altogether, to another country or more preferably, continent. Knowing Boss, he's probably used this opportunity to finally follow his beautiful dream of starting up his own cartel in Mexico. And here I am, strutting around like a beastie boy, thinking he still has people looking for me, so he could exact his revenge. Blah and blah.

The main street takes me to the village centre, marked by a stout little church, a café and a shop. Everything's shut. I find a shady spot just below the church steps, and sit down. I wish I had a sombrero.

I flap my arms as hard as I can, but all this gets me is a few measly feet off the ground. Hardly worth the effort. I land with a heavyhearted thud, look up at the swifts cutting across the sky, sparrows bursting on and off the scene like fireworks, but my eyes are firmly and longingly set on the peregrine falcon, hovering in the high wind, looking down at me, waiting patiently for me to join him for a hunt. I try again, I flap and I flap, I even use the power of my thoughts to lift me that little bit higher up in the air, but all I manage is a couple of feet, maybe three, before falling back onto the hard ground. I am so angry at myself I could cry. I look up at the falcon, and suddenly it dives towards me. I barely have time to think *he's going for a kill*, when it hits my left side with such force it knocks all the air out of my lungs. I feel its talons dig into my flesh and bone, and I scream with pain, not physical pain, I'm not bothered about that, but there's this other pain, unbearable, the shocking pain of betrayal.

'Never took you for a screamer.'

I don't want to open my eyes, but I do it anyway. A tall figure looms against the afternoon sun, throwing a shadow across my face like no ghost ever could. I try to drop all caring about what happens next, but I find that I no longer can. Ghosts cannot shadows cast, and dead girls who choose to come alive cannot choose how to die again.

That's just the way it is.

'Then again, I don't think you ever had a proper chance to scream,' he says. 'With a proper man.'

Miki.

It's Miki.

So it's Miki who's going to spell the end of me, fucking Miki, a bona fide child molester and murderer, and a general abuser of life. Nice one, God.

Miki's holding a gun in his hand, an odd looking semi, hope it's not a home-made sawn-off, prone to going off when least expected. The strangest thing though, is that every time he moves the hand that's holding the gun, my left shoulder explodes in pain. What the–

'You like my harpoon gun?' Ah. Mystery solved.

'Thought it would be a good idea to shoot you first, just in case you felt like getting up to your old tricks.' He yanks the gun and my shoulder fragments into a million red hot pieces. 'See? Much better than bullets. Let's take a walk.' He yanks the gun real hard this time, brings me to my knees. I scramble to my feet as quickly as I can, and follow the pain. 'Smart, Igor. Be a good girl and nothing bad will happen to you.'

Never a less truer word spoken. Miki knows it, and so do I.

SHOWDOWN

'Take me to your Jeep.' I must look surprised, because he laughs like a demon, says, 'Yeah I saw you coming, you little turkey. There's one road in, and you choose to drive on it. No sneaking up for Igor, oh no, she brave, she dangerous, she more clever than everyone else!' He tugs on the fishing line that connects the harpoon to the gun. I clench my teeth as hard as I can, but a little noise still escapes me. 'You know what you are? What you really are? Just another stupid dirty useless *puta*!'

What's with the mixed message. What's up with this Igor here. Is she a boy, or a girl. Is she smart, or a turkey.

'Do you want to know what Boss said to me? He said, find her, fuck her, break her, burn her, leave her in a ditch – do whatever you like with her, as long as she doesn't come out of it alive.'

We reach the end of the village. I turn around and spot a few shadows poking out of the doors and windows. I almost feel hurt no one is moved enough by my seriously fucked-up plight to try and save me. Come on, guys. He only has one harpoon gun.

'All alone, huh?' Miki approaches the Jeep with

extra caution, using me as a human shield. 'Or do you have that filthy little whore Pearl hiding inside, waiting to pounce?' He makes me open all the doors, peers in from behind. 'Don't even think about head-butting me. Don't even consider it. Is that a posh enough word for you, *consider*? Is that how Boss used to speak to you, all big words and poetry in motion?' He smacks my head for no reason. 'I'll show you Boss I will. I'll show you a special treatment.'

He dusts me down for keys. 'Where did you get the Jeep, eh? Did you steal it?' He stares at me for a moment. 'You didn't, did you, you were given it. Eh? Am I right or am I right? Someone was stupid enough to take you in. And you were stupid enough to leave Pearl with them and come down for supplies.' The worst thing about peasants is their infallible common sense. My mum had it. There was no hiding stuff from that woman, providing she was interested enough in your business to make it hers, which she sometimes was. It wasn't so much what she did, but how she did it. Let's say I wanted to steal a doughnut she specifically instructed not to touch till after lunch. So I'd be sitting in the easy chair, method acting a role of a deeply engrossed comic book reader, while keeping a steady eye on the situation until she'd finally leave to have a coffee with our next door neighbour, Rozi the Queen of Scandal. I'd listen out for the sound of the gate closing behind her, make sure she's proper gone before slipping into the larder and grabbing the biggest, fluffiest doughnut of them all, only to find her standing in the middle of the kitchen, her arms folded across her chest, frowning at me with her caterpillar monobrow, not entirely unlike the one sported by Frieda Kahlo. 'I knew you were up to no good. *Put it back*.' She did this sort of thing all the time. The country folk seem to possess this particular instinct when it comes to other people being up to no good. Probably saved their so-called lives for generations, this talent for knowing what others get up to when no one's looking. I guess most peasants are a bit like animals in a way they commune with nature, human and otherwise. This does not make them better than the rest of us. You just need to take one look at Miki here to know that's true.

'Was it urgent, then?' He smacks me again. 'The supplies? You must've needed something bad enough to risk it all by going out. What was it, a medicine? Is someone sick? Maybe that bitch lost her bastard baby, eh? Look at me when I'm talking to you!' This time he slaps me hard across the face. 'Who do you think you are, disrespecting me like that? I see I'm gonna have to teach you a lesson. I was going to have my lunch first, but it'll have to wait now, won't it, because a spoilt little brat like you can't wait to get what's coming to her.' He tugs the line. I follow, until I'm standing pretty much on top of him. He pulls down my trousers. 'No knickers, eh? You must be gagging for it.' I motion at the harpoon, but he laughs. 'You take me for a fool, is that it?' He punches me in the stomach, so hard I barely manage to stay on my feet. 'The harpoon stays in. Down on your back!'

I motion at the harpoon again, he knocks me off balance and I hit the ground, left shoulder first. The pain is so great I must black out for a moment or two, because the next time I open my eyes I see Miki standing above me, his jeans around his ankles, trying to spank his monkey into life. 'Come on, grow nice, grow big, *vamos amigo*, this bitch needs teaching a big lesson.'

I notice that the harpoon suddenly feels lighter and less part of me. The impact of the fall must've pushed the head back into my shoulder when I hit the ground. I close my eyes, start counting to three, then pull the harpoon out on two. It's an excellent trick that works even better when you don't have to do both the counting and the pulling of the harpoon out of your own flesh.

My eyes meet Miki's. He looks surprised, and slightly embarrassed. I bet he didn't feel embarrassed when he was raping that child in the poppy field. I grab the harpoon with both hands and drive it straight up in between his legs.

He falls down like a tree.

I get away from him, crab-like, and watch him squirm around in the dust and blood.

Just like Bella did, before that dog got to her.

'You didn't have to do this!' He's now sobbing like some ugly pervert baby. 'It hurts, it hurts so much, help me, Igor, please, I'll give you money, I have money! I'm bleeding to death, please, Igor, please – listen; Boss gave me load of cash, bought me out of the camp, he paid me to leave, it's all in my truck, have it, have it all, ahhh, it hurts, Igor, help–'

This is the point where I pick up a rock and smash it over his head. That should keep him quiet for a while.

The couple of dogs I saw lurking about earlier on have since been joined by another three. Does five dogs make a pack. Is one Miki enough to feed an entire pack of dogs.

Once my trousers are back on, I patch my shoulder the best I can with what I have – the gauze Charlotte bound my breasts with, an old plastic bag and a couple of greasy pieces of string. The stuff that gangrene is made of. My shirt's fucked, so I have to take Miki's off, with a difficulty so great I almost cry, curl up and die. But it's got to be done. No one's coming to save me. It's all up to me now, same as it ever was, except I never used to care enough to care. Miki's shirt smells of little girls' vaginas, sweet and clean. I throw up into the bushes, put it on, then throw up again.

It's got to be something I ate.

I notice the pain's all but disappeared, as if by magic of the most suspicious sort, like for instance the Devil's magic, or Disney version of a fairy tale. Don't mean to sound ungrateful, but I still prefer the real fairy tale. At least you know where you stand. There's no mercy in the real fairy tale, there's no pretty in pink, no bullshit, and there certainly ain't no a prince, coming to save you on his mighty white steed.

I use the fishing line to tie together Miki's feet and hands, then drag him off into the thicket. I'm thinking I may as well check out his story. See if there is anything in his truck that wants a new owner. Plus, I promised Charlotte the motherfucking beer, and I ain't leaving without. I remember seeing a canvas satchel at the back of the Jeep, so I grab it and shove in the harpoon gun, its handle poking out just enough to warn off the weasely locals, but hopefully not enough to provoke them into doing anything stupid.

It only takes me ten or so minutes to circumnavigate the whole village. I don't find Miki's truck, but I do find a bright red Mercedes half-heartedly hidden underneath a willow tree. Something tells me this is the truck Miki was talking about, but never mind – having a harpoon driven through your scrotum and high up into your gut would probably confuse a man ten times as bright as Miki.

I check it out for any obvious signs of entrapment, like tarantulas or poisonous snakes or landmines. Must admit I'm starting to feel a little edgy, now that the adrenaline's all but left my system. Seriously though, where does the adrenaline go once we no longer need it. Does it return to adrenal glands, for recycling. Or what. I pull the handle and driver's door opens up like a dream. The glove box compartment contains Miki's passport with his ugly mug staring at me accusingly from a page. I notice he was born about half an hour's drive from my so-called home. As far as we both know, we may even be related, or have a friend of a friend in common, six degrees of separation-style. What a terrible thought. I pick up the passport, as well as a charming gold knuckleduster and a small pistol that conveniently came with a box of bullets, and put them into my satchel.

The rest of the car is clean, which means Miki was sleeping somewhere else. Who's the lucky villager, then. And do they have small children. I bet they do, bet they have a nine or ten-year-old daughter, big brown eyes, long wavy hair; I bet Miki touched that hair, again and again, because he could and because no one would stop him.

I try and open the boot but find it's locked. Should've returned the favour and shaken Miki down for keys. I pick up the biggest rock I can carry and smash it against the lock. And again. And again. The boot springs wide open, almost takes my chin with it. A couple of suitcases, full of Miki's clothes, he did love his labels and his shoes and his eau de toilettes and his hairnets. I bet my bottom dollar he was a closeted gay, who insisted on playing the role of this macho woman-banger, before punishing innocent little girls for his subsequent bedroom fiascos. Where I get all the amazing insight from I do not know, all I know is that it sounds true to me.

I toss his clothes onto the ground. No money. I shake the first suitcase, then the other. Although the same size, one seems much heavier than the other. I take the trusted harpoon out of the satchel, use the blood-covered tip to rip open the lining. And surprise, surprise, out come Miki's life's earnings. Wodges upon wodges of British sterling and US dollars. Had no idea Miki was such a traveller, such a world class explorer, such a big motherfucking big spender. I shove the money into the satchel, consider taking the Merc, then decide against it on account of first of all the bad vibe it gave out, and secondly well it wasn't exactly as if I needed to attract any more attention to my wanted person self.

As I walk down the main so-called thoroughfare, I feel like an original superhero again. I bet Miki was a proper pain in their collective peasant arse, a cancer that took over their entire living breathing organism, cancer they had no balls to cure in the only way it could ever be totally cured, which is by ripping it out and feeding it to the dogs. I look around for a suitable hero's welcome, but not one villager comes out to play. The whole place feels different than before, I can sense that the pulse is back on, even though its owners are still hiding behind their mud walls and weathered wooden shutters. Ungrateful bastards they may well be, but truth to be told, I don't really give a shit about them for as long as I get to feel like Superman with another notch carved deep on my gay yellow belt, and feeling dead proud of it.

The café's open, so naturally I want to go in, have a beer like any normal person would, can't remember the last time I bought my own beer in a bar, must have been during my previous incarnation. I walk through one of those plastic multicoloured fly-blinds and enter a dusty room made out entirely of varying degrees of gloom. Judging by the half-opened shutters and a duster left on the bar, I'd hazard a guess someone's left here in a hurry, and not too long ago either. I pat the pistol in my back pocket, for reassurance more than anything else. I don't feel like I'm in mortal danger right now, either because I'm all spent in that department, or my intuition is trying to tell me the worst is over, relax, grab a beer, a handful of savoury snacks, maybe even a bowl of gambas with garlic and paprika, and a few of those delicious fried squid rings on the side. There's a door behind the bar, left ajar. I walk straight over and kick it open. More shadows, and amongst them a flash of bright yellow. I squint harder, work out that it's a dress, attached to a girl, crouching on the floor with her head in her hands, the top part of her body covered in cascades of long black hair. I check the space behind her, full of crates and brooms and other such non-threatening shit. If this girl was my daughter, I'd be storming down this place like a demon, destroying anything or anyone who dared present itself as a threat to her. Seriously. Who are these chicken shit people. Without taking my eyes off her, I reach out into a fridge and grab a couple of beers. I open them with my own teeth, like a proper rascal, then push one over to her.

Slowly, she removes one of the heavy duty locks away from her face, to uncover the biggest roundest blue eye I have ever seen. It is of planetary proportions, her eye. She checks me out, then clocks the beer. Me. Beer. Me; the giant blue rolls up and down like this for a while. I just stand there, drink my beer as if it was my very first and the very last.

Eventually, she straightens up, grabs the bottle and downs its content all in one go. She wipes her mouth with the back of her hand, then jumps to her feet so abruptly, I back into the sink and simultaneously pull out my pistol. We stare at each another for a moment. She burps. I smile. We exchange friendship bracelets.

Okay, the last bit didn't happen. I put the pistol

down on the table, pull out a couple of chairs. We both sit, crack open another bottle of beer. She brings out a box of chocolate-tasting cigarettes (I almost throw up – again; she laughs; I get used to the taste, have one more for luck), and a bag of salty potato crisps of the tastiest kind. She doesn't utter a word. She doesn't even try. She seems to understand that words, they count for nothing.

I wish someone told Pearl.

I pull out a random roll of banknotes and hand it over to her. The pair of the giant blues roll up and down, up to me again. She then smiles and swipes the money off the table. Good girl. Hope she uses it unwisely. I help myself to as many beer bottles as I can carry, and a couple of bottles of Coke, for Ivy and Pearl. Mema always said that Coke wasn't good for you, and I agree. In fact, I agree with her on more things than she'll ever know.

All set to go, I stand in the middle of the floor, thinking how I'd like to tell the girl to get the fuck out of this village, go far, far away, never to return, when she walks over and offers a bag of chewy caramels and a glittery red paper lantern. She then kisses me, and when I say kisses, I mean *kisses*, on the lips, with tongue and everything. I try to move away, but she pulls me closer and holds me tight, before suddenly removing herself in what must be that dramatic-change-of-mind scenario men so love to bitch about and use as a proof that women are an altogether unreliable sex. Well now I get their point.

'Chica?' The girl is staring at my boobs.

So.

She thought I was a boy.

I shrug, she runs back into the storage room.

I must feel extremely offended, because I throw up all over the floor. Never mind. I get a feeling she'd expect no less from her man.

I find the pack of dogs downsized to the original pair. The larger of the two, the one who looks like a cross between Marmaduke and Mr Peabody (hold the glasses), softly growls as I walk by, almost as if he's pleased to see me.

I avoid looking towards the bushes, but in the end I just can't help it, I'm too spooked with the idea that Miki may have survived against all odds, and is now about to pounce and spill his guts and sperm and blood and brains all over me, like a zombie on the loose. So despite already storing enough gruesome images to traumatise a Vulcan, I can't leave without making doubly sure Miki's well and truly gone way down south to the unrighteous land of eternal flames.

I step towards the bushes I had dragged his unconscious body off to, and straight away I hit the ankle-deep pool of blood. I curse and wipe my feet on the clumps of scorched grass, delighted to see the pack has obviously finished off the job I started, albeit in an unbelievably messy pup way. There's blood and random gore everywhere, scattered as far as the passenger's window of my Jeep. Avenging hounds of hell, catching up with the tormentor of their village. I get in and reverse the fuck out. Time to go home. I pull down the sun visor and smile into the mirror. People are right. I do look deranged when I smile.

HEAVEN IS A PLACE ON EARTH

I drive up to the house just as the sun retreats behind the mountain, leaving a deep purple halo in its wake. Night comes next, total darkness, no shades of grey, no lingering technicolour sunsets for lovers' eyes only around here. There's nothing gradual about this part of the world, nothing moderate. It either pours for weeks on end, curtain upon curtain of falling liquid sky, or the sun blisters away day after day, week, after week, month after month. Then without a warning the rain returns. Old people around here are all dressed in black. I used to think they were in mourning, old people are forever losing friends and relatives, it comes with a territory. Now I know they are in mourning, but they are not mourning for others, they are mourning for themselves. Like I said, it comes with the territory. The day comes, maybe their fiftieth or sixtieth birthday, when they take off their browns and blues, give away their reds and greens, and they put on their black suits and dresses, they embrace the role *los candidatos de la muerte* – and then they wait.

People are so weird. Come to think of it, so is my brain. Why the hell would it want to ponder the fashion sense of old people I'll never know, but right now I appreciate how it's almost distracting me from feeling the pounding ache in my temples and the hellfire burning inside my shoulder.

'What the fuck kept you?'

I practically fall out of the Jeep, wounded and half-dead, not to mention thinking I want to be sick yet again *and* wondering if it could be meningitis – and this is the welcome I get.

'It is a simple question,' says Charlotte. 'Are you deaf, as well as dumb?'

I pick myself up off the ground, then charge into her, smashing my fists into her chest and knocking her clean off her drunken-cunt feet. My shoulder explodes into a brand new universe, filled with pretty fluorescent zigzag lines and tiny silver stars. Charlotte moans. I walk back to the track, as gently as can be, collect the loot from the boot and head for the house. Halfway there, I stop and drop the load, then hobble back to Charlotte. Our eyes meet for a moment; I never saw so much fear in someone's eyes. Not even Bella's. I place a bottle of beer on the ground next to her, pause, then add one more.

There really is no place like home.

I'm sitting on a bar stool in the middle of the kitchen, stripped down to my underwear and eating a peach. The juice drips juice all over Pearl, which serves her right for forcing me to strip and sit, so she could patch me up. Turns out I had a few more cuts and bruises than I was aware of, besides the hole in my shoulder that is.

Charlotte's sitting in the armchair opposite me, draining off her second beer. 'I wish she spoke, I really do.'

You seriously don't, you saggy old lady.

'I believe she does speak,' says Pearl. 'She just does not speak in front of other people.'

They talk about me like I'm not even here, like I was a ghost, or worse – a child.

Pearl laughs. 'Look at Igor! She has a face like little baby!'

That little mind-reading Sahara witch.

'I think it's time for this baby to grow up,' says Charlotte. 'One word is all it takes, little Igor.'

For the record, I'm hardly little. The last time Boss measured me – and he did like measuring me, as well as keeping a graph of my periods – I was 173 centimetres tall and weighing fifty-three kilograms. So not exactly short am I. I have no idea what makes people call me little, but I'd rather they didn't. In an ideal world, they wouldn't be calling me anything at all, because my ideal world would be altogether devoid of people and so there would be no need to walk around with a stupid name tag. Only a big bazooka launcher in case I spot a sign of any sci-fi fans. They are such a pain in my ass, such a bore, even bigger pain than hippies. And feminists. And people who are not from India, but still do yoga. This world is full of bores. If Hitler only thought to exterminate all the bores, instead of the Jews and Gypsies, who by the way I just happen to find quite interesting, he would've probably won the war.

'Where did you get the dosh?' Charlotte is smiling

at me, like we're some sort of friends on full smiling terms. She looks a mess, with hair so unwashed it's starting to resemble some stupid white-chick's dreadlocks, and mascara running down both of her nostrils, and a few top buttons missing from her dress, likely to have popped off when I smashed into her earlier on. Hate to admit it, but she somehow still manages to look good, despite all the chaos. I especially like the pretty pale blue slip she's wearing underneath her dress; and what, am I a lesbian now. The best thing, though, is that her eyes have lost that brink of insanity expression she greeted me with upon my arrival. The bad news is the madness will most probably return with a few more beers under her belt, and then again when she comes round afterwards, all sober and nasty and ill. 'Please tell me you haven't robbed some innocent international businessman, if there is such a thing. Look, I even found a roll of liras. Wouldn't it be great to spend it in a small yet exclusive Roman boutique? What do you think, girls? A complete makeover?'

I think of my grey dress, never worn, and clench my teeth. Should've stolen the yellow dress off that girl. Fuck, I wish I thought of it then, instead of wasting my time playing nice.

'My mother did sewing for the family,' says Pearl. 'But she was nasty woman, so all clothes she made scratched and pulled. Me and my sisters hated wearing them.'

'That's a pity,' says Charlotte. 'Is she still alive?'

'No, she passed away.' She air-spits to the side. 'I spit on her grave.'

'Wow,' says Charlotte. 'What has she done to deserve this?'

'She gave me away.' Pearl turns to me. 'All done, little one, but do not move, let the body soak up the medicine.'

'You poor baby,' says Charlotte. 'What about your father?'

Pearl examines her hands, like you do when you'd rather not show and tell. 'Ocean, it took him.'

Charlotte uncorks another beer. 'I hated mine. At least we had one parent to love, which is more than most people. Oh, the humanity… Doesn't it just break your heart?' Well I'm not buying it. Charlotte may seem like a normal person, having a normal conversation, connecting with another human being. But I know that no matter what she says, no matter how charming and interested she appears to be, she doesn't give an actual flying fuck whether you live or die. All she really cares about is having enough booze to take her places no human would dream of visiting, unless they're majoring in earthly explorations of hell. But does Pearl see this? No she does not.

'Yes,' says Pearl. 'I loved my father very much.'

I jump off the stool and pull on my shirt. Someone's shirt. Who cares. We can't all wear pretty silk slips and have our nails done blood-red to match our lips. I grab a pen out of Charlotte's hand – she's writing a list of chores for the rest of us to do whilst she's sleeping it off. 'Hey!' she says, but stops right there. Bet she reckons her chest is plenty bruised enough as it is.

I turn the page, write, AMINA.

'Amina?' Charlotte reads. 'I believe this is Igor's real name!' Do I look like a mother fucking Amina. I tap her stupid forehead, and not too gently, either, then point at Pearl. 'Igor, love, enough with the violence, or I swear I'll get my shotgun and murder you in your sleep!'

Fair enough.

Pearl's smiling in my general direction. 'Oh Igor, you remembered my name.' The next minute she's crying. 'Sorry… It is just, I am so touched.'

Charlotte takes a deep breath, says, 'Come here, girl!' I'm the last person to comment on other people's caring sharing habits, having none of my own and planning to keep it that way, but I must say I do admire Charlotte's ability to make the wounded party walk the entire length of the kitchen floor in order to receive a short stiff hug and a pat on the back akin to a reluctant spot of dusting. This takes some serious style, not to mention cheek.

'There, there,' she says. 'Amina? Would you like me to call you this from now on?'

Pearl nods, all snotty and tearful. 'My mother sold me to those men.'

'Ouch,' says Charlotte. 'What a shame.'

'Yes,' says Pearl. 'It was shame. I had to go. I had to.'

'Of course you did, Amina, dear.'

'What they did to me…' Pearl buries her head in her hands. Quick as lightning, Charlotte grabs a bottle and takes a swig. Our eyes meet, she gives me a wink. 'Animals! But what choice did I have?'

'Well – Amina – it's no good talking about this

now. Much better to let bygones be bygones, you have a new life now, you're free.'

'Yes!' Pearl's eyes light up. 'This is my new life, my chance to say goodbye to old me!' She grabs Charlotte's hand and presses it against her lips. Charlotte looks pained, time to return that wink. 'Thank you, Miss Charlotte, thank you for this opportunity. I shall never let you down! You can trust me. And you do not need to worry about Igor, for I shall keep my eye on her.'

Charlotte starts laughing, causing Pearl to immediately revert to her usual befuddled self. 'Sorry, Amina, didn't mean to startle you. And I appreciate what you're saying, I really do, it's just the look on Igor's face when you said you'd keep your eye on her…'

Pearl checks me out, and there must be something hilarious about the way I'm leaning against the kitchen counter, nursing my beer, doing my best not to puke all over their little bonding play-act, because she too bursts into a fit of giggles. God, how I hate that word.

Ivy enters the kitchen, dressed in her best outfit ever, according to my cunningly hidden exquisite taste for fine things in life. Starting from the top, she's wearing a poppy-red cloche hat with three small white feathers tucked into the black satin ribbon that encircles it. Her skin is pale, but radiant, made even more so by meticulous application of rosebud-pink rouge upon her lips and, less manifestly, cheeks. Now that I've met a few ancient people and understand the necessity behind the invention of the turtleneck top, I appreciate Ivy's choice to tie a dark blue scarf around her own turtleneck. Next comes a light linen shirt, black and long-sleeved, followed by black linen palazzo trousers and bare feet.

'Why is everyone so jolly?' she says. 'It upsets Igor. And if Igor's upset, I'm upset!' She grabs the ceramic candle holder and smashes it against the tiles, then bursts into tears.

Charlotte jumps to her feet. 'Mother!'

'Don't worry, Miss Charlotte, I will take care of her.' Pearl offers Ivy her hand, the old bird grabs it and holds on for dear life. 'Come on, Miss Ivy, let's clean you up.'

It's only then I notice blood dripping down Ivy's left foot. Must've been hit by shrapnel. Silly old fox. Why did she have to go and hurt herself.

Charlotte waits for Pearl and Ivy to leave, before looking me straight in the eye, no trace of drunken haze in her face nor voice. 'Thank you for coming back, Igor.' I feel a grin coming up, what's wrong with me. 'I know I wouldn't.'

Now she tells me.

'I miss my life.' She points at the empty bottles of beer, lined up on the table in front of her. 'This here, this isn't my life, or at least it never used to be. I miss my life, Igor! I miss London, the South Bank, the Photographers Gallery, the Society Club! And the theatre, oh how I miss the theatre! I'd kill for an evening out in London, with a dinner and a play, a man's hand on the small of my back, guiding my way through the night…'

I knew it, I knew there would be a man at the end of that sentence. There always is, especially when it comes to sad old women like Charlotte.

'Hey ho,' she says. 'We're here now, in the middle of this very fine mess, and we must work out the best way forward; and where do you think you're going?'

Feeling agreeably sleepy after drinking all those beers, I was off to have a little snooze in the orchard, what else. And what business is it of hers, anyway.

'Can you please stay for just another minute?' I check Charlotte's face, and unlike me, she seems genuinely interested in what she has to say. Still, I stay and don't exactly prick up my ears. Although not drunk, she must be halfway there and so highly likely to say stuff that sounds important only inside her own pretty little head. And she does look pretty, Charlotte. Mellow, and kind of sassy. Unfortunately for her, I'm not, repeat not, a lesbian, and will not be placing my hand on the small of her back to guide her through the night any time soon this side of forever. 'I know you pride yourself on being a free spirit, Igor, a bit of a maverick. And I can't even imagine what you must've been through, what dire straits you had to negotiate before stumbling across us.' I feel a scratch in my throat, a really deep annoying one. Perhaps I'm getting tonsillitis. I always used to get tonsillitis when I was a child, and it would always start as an innocent little scratch. But a few hours later, I'd be proper struck down with fever, and spend the night hallucinating all over the place. Drove my mum to distraction, she couldn't handle me mad. So she'd take me to the doctors, get them to pump me full of penicillin, despite my profound aversion to needles. Not to mention despite Mema's thorough disapproval of modern medicine. 'You know I have herbs!' she would tell my mum. 'You know you can bring her to me any time, day or night!' And my mum would say, 'She is my daughter! I will take care of her the best way I see fit. Not you – me!' This would lead straight into one of their frequent non-speaking periods, during which I was employed as their messenger pigeon. Flip, flap, I went from Mema to Mum, and back. 'Mema says she's ordering ten chickens from Mrs. Dobrić, cleaned and plucked – would you like some?' 'Mum says she'll have ten also, as long as they are not as skinny as they were the last time.' 'Mema says if you don't like the chickens she gets from Mrs. Dobrić, you are welcome to get yours elsewhere!'

Charlotte's voice brings me back from my reverie, as they would say in a real bad book. 'All I know is that it must've been hard. And that you're here, now, with us. And that Pearl needs our help. I guess what I'm trying to say…' Charlotte laughs. It sounds like a fairy stuck inside a crystal ball. 'In a rather roundabout way – I'm getting on your nerves, correct?'

I nod.

She laughs again. The crystal ball breaks, the fairy flies away. 'I'm asking you to please, please consider staying put until Pearl has her baby. Having you around would make the whole thing far less stressful for her, and therefore easier for everyone.'

I sit there, feeling the pressure.

'Please, Igor.'

The pressure mounts.

'We're very fond of you, do you know that?'

I try and make myself think.

'Especially Pearl.'

The easiest thing would be to say yes, then get the fuck out of the kitchen, run down to the orchard, be alone for a change. So I say yes, I nod.

'Thank you,' says Charlotte. 'Thank you so much. Shall we shake on it?'

Well as long as they don't expect me to get involved with the horrible not to mention totally unnecessary event of Pearl giving birth to her ugly baby. Not even boiling the water. I refuse.

Charlotte takes my hand. Her handshake is firm, yet feathery. Messenger pigeon, meet the white dove from above.

CHARLOTTE

It's not like I'm hurting anyone, is it? All right, perhaps myself, a tad, but I believe that the benefits vastly outweigh any alleged harm. I simply know this to be true. No point in trying to explain this to others. They would never understand. How could they? They are only children, and lost ones at that. Amina may catch up, eventually, once her child is born. But Igor, she is lost inside-out. And as for Mother… I haven't seen Mother for days, I fear she might have gone forever. What am I meant to do with the empty shell she has left behind? I wish I could just run away, never to return. Yes. I ought to simply turn around and walk away from these empty shells, from this unforgiving land, from this barren life, from myself.

CURED

I'm finding it hard to get through a day. It's fine when I'm asleep, give or take a hairy dream, but eventually I have no choice but to confront the infinite stretches of time that demand to be navigated. By me, of all people. What to do; what to do. The getting drunk option is out of equation, thanks to Charlotte's latest rampage which involved a bottle of bourbon, a short but electrifying demonstration of Norman Bates' knife-wielding skills, and several attempts of burning down the house with a DIY torch I had innocently watched her make out of a wooden dowel, an old cotton shirt and a can of paraffin. Must admit I was totally impressed at first, but I quickly changed my mind when I caught her putting the lit torch to the curtains in Ivy's bedroom, while singing a jolly French song in a creepy deadpan voice. I don't spook all that easy, but Charlotte, singing like that, and just standing there, coolly observing the flames deliberately scaling the folds of the fabric, it scared the shit out of me. Plus it brought back this eerie Indiana image of some idiot girl in a mental institution*, an unlovely child to put it politely, with a head of an old woman and a bandaged finger, and altogether one of those things you really wish you never saw, but you did and now you're stuck with it for the rest of your life. There was this boy once, yeah, in my previous so-called existence, who had made it his life mission to try and impress me, mostly by giving me random pretentious stuff he presumed my dreams were made of, like for instance the book which contained the image of the idiot girl. It was written by some French so-called philosopher, and I hated the book, and I hated the boy who had given it to me, and most of all I hated that idiot girl for being such an idiot. But I digress. In the end, Charlotte managed to knock herself out by slipping on the paraffin covered tiles, and now all the drink is gone and I'm left with fuck all to do. Except watch over Pearl. Which is as stimulating as having sex with a copy of one of Virginia Woolf's novels, except even less so.

I manage to waste a reasonable chunk of time searching for the hidden booze, until Pearl finds me snooping through Ivy's knicker-drawer and, whilst totally missing out on the most excellent opportunity to poke merciless fun at my predicament, informs me that she had personally removed every last drop of alcohol from the house, as well as its grounds. 'I hid one bottle of cough mixture underneath first step leading up to veranda, in case someone gets bad throat. I also hid Miss Ivy's best perfume, but the rest is gone, every single last drop.'

I wait until she takes her self-righteous Sahara ass back to the kitchen where it belongs, then scuttle off outside. The top part of the step comes off easily, without a squeak. Not that I'm afraid of getting caught. It's just that I generally prefer to get away with my crimes, let someone else take the blame. Like for example stupid bloody Charlotte. It's her fault we've all gone Alcoholics Anonymous, even though it's only her who has a problem holding her liquor. How is that even fair.

I unscrew the top off the cough mixture, quickly screw it back again. It smells vile, like Frankenstein's monster's idea of a banana. I refused to drink this shit when I was two, I'm not about to start now. I find Ivy's perfume straight away, stashed away under her bed. Pearl either makes for a shitty hider, or her tagine was burning so she had to ahem think with I repeat *with* her feet. I inspect the blue crystal bottle attached to a purple atomizer. Almost full, and very pretty. So pretty in fact, my hand hovers hesitantly over it. My head says, 'Rip it apart! Drink it out of spite – you know it makes sense!' But my hand won't do it. And besides, my throat suddenly feels so tight I very much doubt I'd be able to swallow a drop. I sigh. What am I now, sentimental.

I lie on the ground. The earth underneath me is soft and crumbly, like a freshly dug out grave. I want to stay here forever, lying face down in this earth at the bottom of the lemon grove. But this crying, it has got to stop. People who say that crying's good for you have obviously never had a proper cry in their entire life. Snotty-sleeve criers, the handkerchief dabbers, the storm in a cup, cry me a river brigade. They have no idea. But I do, and I say: crying isn't good for you.

Eventually, I stop. All I feel now is anger, so it's all back to normal, thank fuck. I came down here to pick a few lemons, as you do when you have nothing else to do, but then my stomach started to hurt so bad I thought I was about to get hit with the worst case of diarrhoea known to mankind. I even took off my shorts and everything, when a particularly mighty cramp doubled me up onto all fours, and suddenly I found myself howling like a dingo. I have never heard a dingo howl, not even on *Survival*, but I'm sure that's how it felt to me, I was howling like a proper outback dingo, baring my teeth and I'm almost tempted to say *my soul*, for all to see. But now, despite the anger, I actually feel peaceful. I mean, not at all violent. And also kind of tired. I look for a tree with the longest shade, then sit with my back against its smooth bark, and moments later, I'm going, going, gone.

Ivy's face floats in front of my eyes, like an après-party helium balloon, still bursting with colour but sagging fast round the edges.

'Good morning, Igor,' she says, then runs off.

I shake my head a little, like a dog, or rather like a dingo. Where am I. A lemon hits the ground to my left. Then another. Is it raining lemons. The next one gets my leg, clearly this is not a case of ripe fruit falling into my lap, it's a case of someone throwing lemons at me. I'm under a full blown attack. I jump to my feet, trying not to panic. Come on. Doubt Boss would waste time by throwing fruit at me. Unless he actually would.

I growl and break into a mad dash amongst the trees. I zig and I zag, catch me if you can, whoever you are, until I practically crash into Ivy, standing in the middle of a clearing, cradling a pile of lemons in the skirt of her white linen dress. 'What the fuck, Ivy!' I want to say, except I can't, can I. This dumbness of mine, it really can be a double-edged sword.

Ivy screeches with excitement. 'I've been caught! I've been naughty, and now I've been caught!'

I rub my leg. It feels hot and bruised. And where the hell is Pearl, she's supposed to look after the old dame. Not me, her. I have no choice but to fold Ivy's arm under mine and start marching her up the hill, towards the house.

'What will be my punishment?' she asks. 'How will you punish me, my dear, handsome, horrible Igor? Will you kiss me?'

She purses her lips in my general direction. Seriously not in the mood for this. Alright, I can't very well blame Ivy for wanting me, but I do blame her for trying to do something about it. Pearl of course thinks this is hilarious. Considering she once laughed for at least one hour after she noticed her left foot was slightly bigger that her right, Pearl's sense of humour leaves a lot to be desired, is all I'm saying.

It takes some persuading, whilst simultaneously dodging her roguish advances, but in the end I manage to get Ivy standing on the veranda step like a good girl she clearly doesn't wish to be.

'What shall we do now?' she asks me. 'Can we do something bad? Let's do a really bad thing, Igor, let's break a plate!'

I feel like crying again. Sentimental and depressed, what's up with me these days. One thing I do know, I don't want to be bad. Never did. But I don't want to be good either.

Charlotte is sitting in her usual spot, under the pale-blue parasol, staring into middle distance, looking as limp and dejected as a retired porn star's dick. How very attention seeking of her. And where the fuck is that lazy, good for nothing slave girl. I give Ivy a little shove towards the kitchen, but she won't budge. Her eyes are glued on her daughter, and, horror of horrors, rapidly filling up with tears. I grunt and give her another push. Go on, Ivy. Forward march.

'Igor.' Ivy's voice suddenly sounds just like her daughter's. 'Charlotte is fading away. She needs some colour. Will you fetch it for her, please?'

Days get easier as they turn into weeks. Perhaps time really can heal everything, including boredom. I even achieve something of a daily routine, which is rich, coming from me. But the very fact it's coming from me, not anyone else, must count for something. True, I was kind of forced to stumble across this house, but it was my choice to stay until after the arrival of Rosemary's baby. No one tells me what to do any more, not even my so-called inner demon. I open my eyes, and I'm pretty much free to do whatever I feel like, aside from an occasional house chore. God I hate chores. What a waste of my time, and humiliating too. I try my best to avoid them, of course, but no matter how good I am at being invisible, Pearl's eye still homes in on me like a deadly all-seeing missile.

'The rubbish bin needs emptying,' she says. 'You can see it needs emptying. Who do you think will empty it? Me? Do you expect me to do everything around here, eh?'

Jesus woman, no cry. It's only a bloody rubbish bin, and not a very full one at that.

Chores aside, I do what I want when I want. Except at meal times, which are so strict they frankly put me right off my food. So for example, we must sit down to breakfast at 8 o'clock sharp, or go hungry. Another one of Pearl's brightest, of course. I bet she only invents all these rules so she can boss me about even more. I mean, what's she going to do if Ivy suddenly decides she wants to eat her breakfast at 8.45. Fuck all, is what. But if I'm only a minute late, she goes berserk, in that holier-than-thou way of hers that makes me want to punch her on the head. 'Time waits for

No one,' she goes. 'If you're not here for 8 o'clock, then you will just have to wait until midday for your next meal.'

Just as well I'm a morning person then. We eat freshly baked bread with home-made strawberry jam I have a love-hate relationship with it because I'm usually the one who ends up making it all by myself. Watching the pan so it doesn't burn, stirring it for hours on end, trying it for the right consistency, and all because Pearl is allegedly attending to a business elsewhere. Or my favourite, toasted day-old bread sprinkled with salt and olive oil, then rubbed with freshly picked tomatoes from the garden. We have ham and eggs on Sundays only, supposed to be a special treat but I don't really like Sundays so it's hard for me to find anything special about that. Except for an early morning visit to the chicken coop. Never thought I'd say this, but chasing the chickens and stealing their eggs is probably one of the most exciting things I've ever done. Not convinced that's the actual proper way of doing it, but it's hardly my fault no one's ever bothered to show me the ropes. All Charlotte said was to give the cock a wide berth, which made me laugh all the way to the coop. I only stopped laughing when I met the fucker and realised I'm facing the meanest, ugliest beast I've ever come across, except maybe for Miki. Saying that, we do have fun. He chases me, I chase the chickens, we all run and fly and hop around in circles, screaming and clucking and feathers flying all over the place. The Girl Who Ran With The Chickens. How's that for a tombstone teaser.

Pearl has rationed up the food in the larder to last us for another couple of weeks. After that, I guess someone will just have to go down to the village again. I don't care who, as long as it ain't me. I get it why Ivy wouldn't make it, and suppose Pearl can be excused on account of her so-called condition, but I don't see why Charlotte couldn't take her perfectly manicured finger out and do something useful for a change. She hasn't had any booze for a couple of weeks now, which obviously means she's totally cured. The shakes are gone, she's eating again. Getting her strength back, as old people would say. Alright, she does seem a bit down, sitting around staring at random empty spaces, but as everyone knows nothing beats the depression quite like a trip to the shops.

After breakfast, I'm double quick to bugger off before anyone remembers to give me a chore. I run like the wind through the orchard, until I reach the four large grey rocks at the westernmost edge of the garden. And there, twinkling in the morning sun, is my secret pond, served in a perfectly smooth stone bowl of say six metres in diameter. And when I say *my* and *secret*, I mean I seem to be the only person getting any joy out of it. No one else bothers: Ivy's not allowed, Pearl's always too busy, or so she claims, and Charlotte's feeling too sorry for herself to do anything fun these days.

'This is my sacred place,' she told me the day she had first brought me here. It was the morning after the night before, but she seemed to be taking it well. It was only later when I cottoned on she was swigging from a hipflask all along, a hair of a dog that in Charlotte's case inevitably turned into a werewolf come the nightfall, sometimes sooner. I looked around, and had to admit that, if I were a hippy, I guess that's exactly what I'd call this place. Sacred, magic, cosmic, blissful, and other holy shit like that.

The rocks stand tall and wide, like four gay rugby players in a scrum. There is only one entrance, facing southeast, so at this time of the morning, with the sunshine pouring straight into the pond, you end up bathing in the cool clear water *and* the golden sunshine *and* the bright blue sky all at the same time. 'Always choose the highest religion you can find,'

Mema used to say. 'And there's nothing higher that the elements. Choose nature, and it'll choose you back. The returns will be eternal.'

I strip off and jump in. The cold takes my breath away, but in no time I'm breathing again, full and deep, and feeling far more alive than my usual pretend to be dead. I swim around like a shark, ten circles in one direction, then ten in the other, so I don't get dizzy and drown.

And when I get bored, I just float around on my back, like a starfish on holiday.

And through a gap between rugby players' shoulders, I watch the sky watching me.

And I rest in the knowledge that the rest of the day will bring precisely nothing new, no surprises, no information, and no revelations.

Soon, I'll dry off in the sun, snooze a little I bet, then walk up the orchard path back to the house for lunch. Tinned sardines with hard sheep's cheese, tomatoes, a hard-boiled egg maybe. Peaches from the orchard, sprinkled with sugar and grilled, if Pearl's in the mood. Afterwards, I'll sit on the veranda and read. I found this knackered copy of *Gösta Berling's Saga* by Selma Lagerlöf, which I must admit brought up a lot of annoying feelings not to mention memories about my so-called previous life, which was filled with literature and music and other useless stuff. But I managed to push it all down again, and enjoy the read from the vantage point of my current incarnation as Mad Dog Slayer (on the run), with the word mad referring to the dog, not the slayer.

At 4pm, we drink coffee and eat fresh figs, or a

piece of almond cake, then start preparing supper, which is served at 6pm. I always help, not because I want to, obviously, but because Pearl sends me off to the garden to pull carrots, pick grapes and gather herbs, or maybe she'd give me a mountain of spinach to sort through.

'It may look like a mountain to you,' she'd say, reading my thoughts again like a proper rude girl. 'But remember, Igor, spinach *wilts*.'

As if I have room in my brain for such information. Spinach what. Spinach wears kilts. Oh right. Who would've thought.

After supper, we normally listen to random old-fashioned records. Charlotte and Ivy don't even own a TV, let alone a video player. Must admit, I miss watching movies. The first thing I'm going to do when I get out of here, providing I ever do, is go to the cinema. I don't care what's showing – I'll watch anything. An afternoon matinee double bill of anything. Jett can come if he wants to, and we'll share a bag of oversalted popcorn. Later on, we'll step out on the rainy street of some big city, and he'll put his coat over our heads, and we'll stand on a kerb, hail a cab. Or run across the road to the nearest coffee shop. Or maybe a bar. It's a work in progress.

Ivy usually dances to all the tunes, round and round she goes, again and again until she's bushed. I join in when the mood takes me; Charlotte used to, but only when she was pissed. It was fun, all of us prancing about like we did, but I'm glad that her drinking days are over. She was becoming a right nuisance to be around, and a crying shame to watch, stumbling and slurring about the place like some sad fallen angel who cut off her own wings and traded them in for a bottle of cheap bourbon. I guess this must've been extra hard on Ivy and Pearl who chose to remain stone cold sober throughout The Many Rampages of Charlotte. Not me, of course, I always managed to sneak in a few without anyone noticing. Even after Pearl took to hiding the booze; especially then.

Hiding and finding of the bottles became a bit of a slapstick theatre for a while, and it went something like this: first act, Pearl would confiscate all the bottles she could find and hide them behind the jam jars on the bottom shelf in the larder. Second act, Charlotte would promptly locate them, drink as much as she could, then squirrel the rest all over the house. Third act, Pearl would be handing Ivy a crudely drawn map of the place.

'You find a bottle, any bottle, and you bring it to me,' she would say. 'Whatever you do, do not give a bottle of alcohol to your daughter. To Charlotte. Do not give her a bottle. Do you understand?'

Ivy would squeal with delight at the prospect of a new adventure, then skip off far too sprightly for a woman with one foot already stuck in the grave. One day, Ivy unearthed four bottles of spirits and brought them straight over to Charlotte. By the time Pearl showed up, both Charlotte and I were already pissed as newts, with me screeching like a banshee on LSD as backing vocals to Charlotte's extremely punky rendition of 'Bandiera Rosa', and Ivy crouching in the corner with her hands pressed against her ears.

'You should be ashamed of yourself, Igor!' Pearl told me off, as if:

a) I was a child, and

b) any of this was my fault.

All in all, Charlotte proved to be an overall winner. She clearly had her own stash planted all over the place, because one moment she'd be talking to you as normal, but the next moment, she'd appear as drunk as a skunk, with that last clandestine swig finally derailing the rest of the runaway train. So yeah, Charlotte may be feeling a little gloomy right now, but I'm guessing it beats cirrhosis of the liver like, hands down. Unless of course she ends up topping herself, in which case I take back what I said about cirrhosis of the liver. If you have to go out, you may as well go out on a piss.

Back in the pond, I suddenly feel a shadow upon my person, and manage to snap out of my starfish just in time to avoid a body hitting the exact spot where my head used to float only a split second ago.

Boss.

Living with fear is one thing, you get used to it, and you learn how to get on with your life regardless of how scared you might be feeling at any given time. It is far worse to live a peaceful life, going around your business like there's no tomorrow, then getting punched in the chest by some unforeseen fearful event. Bet that's how you get a heart attack. Bet it's a miracle I didn't get one just now.

A head pops out of the water, says, 'I'm so glad I found you, dear Igor! My daughter Charlotte is fading away. You must save her.' Ivy pinches my left cheek. Facial cheek, I hasten to add. 'Now turn around, cutie pie, I'm butt naked and I don't wish to lead you on. No time for romance, you see, because we need to go back to the house and help get Charlotte back to life.'

Ivy, not Boss.

So why am I not relieved.

BABY GOD

I like a good bookcase. A book presented on a flimsy bookcase isn't a book I'd want to read. Two entire walls in Charlotte's study are fitted with sturdy walnut bookcases similar to those in Big Daddy's library. My heart skips a beat. I feel guilty. What the hell am I feeling guilty about now. I stop to think, whilst scanning the books lined up on those beautiful shelves like Red Army soldiers on the 1st of May parade. Then it dawns on me; I haven't spoken to Mema for days, maybe even weeks. Ever since I returned from my village adventure, in fact. I used to speak to her all the time, she was in everything I saw and heard and tasted. She was the woman standing beside the road, waving me on with a silk blue scarf. She was the child dancing in the middle of the village square, laughing like a baby chimera composed from two-parts Tinkerbelle and one-part common crow. She was the thin golden pancake, filled with apple sauce and cinnamon custard Pearl fed us this morning.

Except that she wasn't. Mema, I mean – she wasn't anywhere near that pancake. I have completely forgotten about her, is the truth. I let the easy life in this house get to me, and take my Mema away.

'So you want to act as this big spoiled brat, eh?' Mema said to me the very last time I saw her. 'Well just remember, if you dance with the devil, the devil doesn't change.'

And what the fuck's that supposed to mean. Nice one, Mema, leaving me with the crappiest last words ever. My eyes suddenly begin to sting, and before I know it, I'm taking off my clothes and hiding in the darkest corner of the study, with my head laid on my knees, crying like no one's baby.

I slam the book on the table in front of Charlotte. Pearl of course gasps, Ivy claps her hands. Without bothering to look up, Charlotte pushes the book away. I pick it up and let it drop onto her plate – I made sure she finished eating the most of her French toast first, I'm not exactly a monster. Charlotte jumps to her feet and for one tiny moment there's a chance I might get punched, but instead she turns away and marches off in that clippity-cloppity fashion beloved by all drama-queens and ponies of this world.

'*Waiting for Godot*,' reads Pearl. 'Who is this Godot? Is he like a baby-god?'

The next time I attempt to interest Charlotte in the book, she chucks it into the evilest brambles ever. I spend the next fifteen minutes recovering it, eventually emerging:

a) victorious,

b) mauled to shreds, and

c) pretty sure the three of us could put up this play without Charlotte's help, after all.

'You want me to read this book to you?' says Pearl. 'What is it with you, Igor, now you want me to be your nanny, as well as a cook?'

'*Je refuse*!' Ivy turns her back to me. '¡*No pasarán*!'

Well I never said it was going to be easy.

That evening, I wait for everyone to gather up on the veranda, before dragging a large, not to mention heavy terracotta pot, housing a tall pink-blossom oleander tree, into the centre. Next, I write a name of the character on an individual piece of paper, then place Vladimir closest to the pot, Pozzo next to him, I suspend Godot in the branches of the tree, and scatter Estragon, Lucky and Boy about as I please.

'What are you up to?' Pearl could hardly sound more suspicious if she tried. 'Better make sure you pick up all the paper off that floor when you are done playing!'

Charlotte chortles. Almost worth forgiving Pearl her stupidity, this little noise. Means Charlotte's paying attention equals means she may join in equals means she'll stop fading away equals means Ivy will quit dogging me like a ghost with a bone.

And then I'll be free. And once I'm free, I'm out of here. For good.

After Pearl's had her baby, obviously.

I open the book at the start of Act I and leave it on the table. Charlotte glances across, but Pearl's already all over it, like the black Sahara plague Camus wrote about, the one that never really goes away, no matter what you do. I return to my makeshift stage with a heavy sigh, sit down next to the sheet of paper with

Estragon written across it, and start pulling off a knackered green wellington boot I found lying around in the barn. What I really wanted was a pair of plain brown boots, but I guess Charlotte and Ivy just ain't the brown boot type. What I did find, how-very-ever, was this secret cupboard packed with the maddest collection of shoes I'm ever likely to meet: red leather shoes, crystal-encrusted shoes, silk green sandals, patent-white stilettos, snake skin slip-ons, and zillion others. Best of all, there amongst all the foot gear, nestled a bottle of vodka, still one-third full. Thank you, baby Godot.

'Igor is playing,' says Ivy. 'With an old welly.' Her eyes are flickering like two shiny new marbles, you can tell the curiosity's killing the old cat. Come on, come on, no time to be shy, let's get this party started, isn't this what you wanted, you moody old dude. Eventually, she gets off her bony ass, smooths down her emerald linen dress, takes a few steps towards me. 'No! Igor doesn't share his toys. I shall not be playing with him today.'

Just as well I got myself a little tipsy prior to this spirited not to mention ingenious attempt at waking Charlotte out of her self-induced coma, is all I'm saying. I continue to fiddle with the boot like a pro, pretending I'm struggling to pull it off, grimacing in pain, wiping the sweat off my brow. Must say, acting comes easily to me. Perhaps I should go to Paris, find myself a little job at the back of a bistro and save all my money for acting classes. Perhaps I should become a famous French theatre star.

'*Wiliwiliwiliwiliwiliwili!*' screeches Pearl. 'I think

Igor is acting! Look!' She shoves the book in front of Charlotte's mulishly turned-up nose. 'It says here, *Estragon, sitting on a low mound, is trying to take off his boot. He pulls at it with both hands, panting* – that is exactly what Igor has been doing for last couple of minutes!'

Feeling not unlike a circus animal done well, I start making pained little noises, acting as if the boot's murdering my foot, and looking towards Vladimir's placemat for assistance. With a corner of my eye, I notice Ivy edging towards the stage, pretending not to. I point at the boot with my index finger, whimpering tenderly into my sleeve.

'What?' Ivy creeps a little closer still, but keeps glancing towards Charlotte. 'Are you in pain, dear Igor? Oh my, oh my, what is one to do?'

I open my arms towards her lazy good for nothing daughter, and do some additional whimpering. Then I wait. And wait. And wait some more, about ten minutes altogether. By which time I'm bored. Who knew acting could be this boring. And uncomfortable; all this sitting on hard floors, whilst handling smelly old boots and reciting your way through the night, every night, for weeks on end. Sorry, theatre goers, you'll just have to come and adore me on the screen of your nearest cinema instead. Movie-making looks to me like heaps more fun anyway, all you do is shoot for like fifteen minutes, then you're free to go back to your trailer and eat salt beef on rye and watch *Betty Blue* for like, the hundredth time.

'Cut it out, Igor,' says Charlotte. 'Can't you see you're scaring mother?'

Happy that finally I got her attention, I open my mouth and let out, 'Boot!'

Not sure what happened next. All I remember is someone jumping to their feet with such vigour they overturned the table. Another someone burst into tears. Or maybe that one was on me. I'll never know. By the time I catch up with my so-called self, I'm already at the bottom of the orchard, lying face down on the ground, listening to the crazy drumming of my own heart, hearing every word it beat.

The next morning finds me wide awake. I never slept a wink, and still I dreamt about traversing sharp mountains and negotiating piranha-infested rivers in search of a lost little boy, and never ever resting until I found him, safe and sound. Not sure if any piranhas actually featured, per se, but the water's turbulent belly sure looked capable of hiding all sorts of badass critters. Equally unsure how I could dream whilst still wide awake, what's that all about. Maybe my consciousness developed a leak that's causing my dreamworld to enter my erm *reality*. Or did it go the other way around.

I sit up. My beady-eyed reflection floats into view through the mirror someone nailed to the wall opposite. Not convinced this is terribly feng shui. Ghosts like to use mirrors to enter human dimension, and haunt us. Especially when we're asleep. I jump out of bed and throw a sheet over the mirror.

Seriously.

Do I really have to think of everything around here.

I return to bed, feeling dead out, yet too restless to sleep the day away. Being human is a tiresome business. Everything's after us, one way or another, the other humans are after us, I don't even trust my own self not to be after me. No wonder I have difficulties sleeping. I wish I was born an animal, almost any animal would do as long as it's not a dog. Talking of which, well sort of, I once watched this episode of *Survival*, about wildlife's sleeping habits. Bats and possums slept like all the time, because they were safely tucked inside their caves and hollow trees. Prey species, like antelopes, they barely ever slept, and even when they did, their noses and ears kept twitching about for any signs of a predator. Don't recall the presenter mentioning anything about whether or not antelopes dreamt, but I bet they did, I bet they dreamt about being a possum, sleeping its life away in some abandoned rocky crevice, dreaming of being an antelope.

I decide to make my appearance at the kitchen table for two reasons only:
  a) my bedroom's starting to annoy me, and
  b) I'm starving hungry.
'Good morning, Igor!'
In unison. As everyone knows, the only time you get two or more women saying anything in unison is when they have something to hide. In this case, my guess is their delight, not to mention excitement, over the fact I went and said my first word last night, in case it spooks me into returning straight back into my shell. Which by the way is exactly what I plan to do. I thought about it,

and I seriously doubt I have what it takes to make it as an actress anyway, too many sexual favours to perform on your way up, too many directors barking orders at you along the way, could spell disaster for everyone involved. Better off minding my own business some place safe and warm and moist and, ideally, free from any outside influences. A place like a womb, preferably not attached to no mother. God, how I wish I was a possum.

I sit in my chair, without looking up, at least not in an obvious way. I do of course take in the general lay of the land, enough to confirm they are all making an effort to act as normal as possible, even poor Ivy, who keeps looking at me, then opening her handbag and whispering into its interior. Charlotte seems proper back in charge, smiling and chatting about the weather with Pearl. And all it took was one word. People are suckers for words.

There's lots of food on the table today. Eggy bread and spicy salami and little gherkins, and those tiny little doughnuts Pearl usually serves for our afternoon tea, still warm and sprinkled all over with vanilla sugar. I eat as much as I can as quickly as I can, because frankly, this cloak and dagger business is starting to get to me. I wish one of them would just come out and say, 'Play it again, Igor, please say *boot*.' I would of course do no such thing, but at least it would be out in the open, and we could all get on with our so-called lives. I lick my plate clean, just to annoy Pearl, then get up to take it to the sink. Can't wait to get away from these maddening crows and float around my secret pond for the rest of the day.

'Igor.'

"What now, Miss Charlotte," I think, but I'm secretly relieved I have a reason to stare openly at her face, like a stalker with a backstage pass. I noticed there was something different about her back at the table, but couldn't give her a full once over on account of not wishing to engage with their conspiracy against me. But now, it's confirmative: Charlotte must've had a spot of overnight plastic surgery, especially inside her eyes, because they look illuminated with a warm golden glow, as if someone's planted a ray of sunshine, or at least a tiny light bulb, behind them. I swear, if it turns out I'm a lesbian, I'm going to kill myself. And then I'm going to go for it.

So now we're all involved in putting on the bastard play. Charlotte's bossing everyone around like no wardrobe and make-up person I've ever heard of.

'Pearl, fetch me that long white wig from the attic, and make sure you don't shake it too much.'

'What about spiders?' asks Pearl. 'Attics are full of spiders.'

'I once found a spider inside my wig,' says Ivy. 'A tarantula.'

'Ay!' Pearl runs her fingers through her golden locks. 'How big was it?'

Ivy opens her arms as wide as they would go.

'Mother! You're not helping!'

Pearl laughs. 'Miss Ivy! Are you humouring me?'

'Why I believe I am,' says Ivy. 'For I am the humorous one!'

Charlotte claps her hands. 'Talking of humorous,

time to get back to our play. Pearl – to the attic, and remember to give the wig only the gentlest of shakes!'

'Right away, Miss Charlotte,' says Pearl. 'Back in one eye blink!'

'Igor!' Charlotte calls. I ignore her. 'Igor? Did you look at the script? The part I pointed out, Lucky's speech?' I ignore her some more. 'Igor?' Her voice turns marshmallow soft. 'I just know you are going to make a perfect Lucky! Please, my love, take a look at the speech when you get a minute, see if you can give it that unique Igor-treatment, turn it into something new.' I know she's playing me, but still I snatch the script out of her hands. 'Great! And when you finish reading, go and help Ivy with the background, make sure she sticks to painting the cardboard only, there's a good girl.'

These stage people, bloody hard to say no to and impossible to shake off, once they've cajoled the first yes out of you. Even Pearl raises a bushy eyebrow or two at the sheer amount of work Charlotte's expecting us to do, and Pearl is a slave girl, dead keen on all things laborious. I read the page with Lucky's speech. She must be having a laugh. First of all, I'm not saying *quaquaquaqua*. Secondly, I'm not acting it, either. As a matter of fact, I'm getting myself the hell out of here, and out of Charlotte's bewitching ways. What was I doing, creating another monster, what's up with that. I throw the manuscript in Charlotte's general direction, and head for the house – and the rest of the vodka.

'Oh come on, Igor, this was your idea!' Charlotte shouts after me. 'And it's fun! Please don't leave!'

As Charlotte's not very lucky stars would have it, looks like all leaving has been cancelled for the foreseeable future, what with Pearl blocking the doorway, blood pouring down her face and chest, turning her pretty white tunic crimson. Must've been one hell of a spider, is all I'm saying.

BOSS

Para bailar La Bamba
Para bailar La Bamba
Se necessita una poca de gracia
Una poca de gracia
Para mi, para ti, ay arriba, ay arriba
Ay, arriba arriba
Por ti sere, por ti sere, por ti sere
Yo no soy marinero
Yo no soy marinero, soy capitan
Soy capitan, soy capitan
Bamba, bamba
Bamba, bamba
Bamba, bamba, bam
Para bailar La Bamba
Para bailar La Bamba
Se necessita una poca de gracia
Una poca de gracia
Para mi, para ti, ay arriba, ay arriba
Para bailar La Bamba
Para bailar La Bamba
Se necessita una poca de gracia
Una poca de gracia
Para mi, para ti, ay arriba, ay arriba

Ay, arriba arriba
Por ti sere, por ti sere, por ti sere
Bamba, bamba
Bamba, bamba
*Bamba, bamba…**

* *La Bamba is a Mexican folk song, originally from the state of Veracruz.*

GODOT RISING

'Forget the apple pie, then,' I said. 'What about chocolate?'

'Which one?' asked Mema.

'Eurocream?'

'As tempting as it sounds, I'd have to decline.'

I frown hard. 'Fruit and nut?'

Mema shakes her head. 'No. You may as well give up.'

'Never!' I watched Mema perform the extraction of the last bits of marrow out of a bone so large I couldn't help thinking it came from one of the *Survival* animals, like an elephant or a hippo. It was blobby and grey and greasy, and I thought Mema must be bonkers to prefer this to chocolate. With a dessert fork, she placed a small amount of marrow on a piece of fluffy white bread, then added a few salt flakes and a smidgen of horseradish. 'You are a little bit disgusting, Mema, did you know?'

'Mmmmm…' Mema closed her eyes and chewed, long and slow.

'Are you sleep-eating again, Mema?' I asked. 'Don't you go and choke, you greedy girl!'

Eventually, she opened her eyes, patted her little

round belly full of things like bone marrow, carps' heads and chicken feet, and said, 'I am now ready for a piece of chocolate. What have you got?'

But I had nothing. 'It was just a theatrical question. I don't actually carry chocolate bonbons in my pocket, you silly billy!'

'Theatrical, eh?'

'Yes. You know, like a test.'

'And have I passed?'

'Yes you have, Mema, you definitely are a gristle girl.'

The hole in Pearl's head is like a car crash, I don't really want to look, yet I'm unable to take my eyes off of it. Located just above her right temple, it spurts out blood in jerky intervals, like a faulty fountain in a village square. Any village would do. As long as it's not this village.

Ha-ha.

'Something funny, eh?' Boss runs his fingers through my hair. 'You strange little thing. I missed you so much.'

Blood. How much blood is there in an average human body. The way Pearl's going, I reckon she'll be drained pretty soon. Somebody do something. But who. I look around the veranda. Charlotte is lying in her very own personal pool, so maybe not her. Ivy's lying in a pool of blood also, with a bullet hole in her chest, so definitely not her. Silly Ivy, she went for them with one of her paint brushes.

'Sorry, Boss,' says a man with a smoking gun in his hand. 'I thought she was coming at me with a bread knife!'

A bread knife. So specific. Must be telling the truth then. Only liars skim over such details. Or is it they embellish them half to death, to cover up the fact they're lying. I will need to look it up, some day. Today seems highly unlikely. Not a great day for research I don't think, well not any more it isn't.

'You thought? With what, exactly?' Boss surveys the scene of his latest crime. 'What a pity, eh, what a shame. I was looking forward to watching Igor tear his captors to shreds, ay, never mind.' Boss stops molesting my hair, but leaves his hand resting on my shoulder. Like we're mates, watching a game of basketball, or whatever it is that mates do together. Keep each other out of harm's way. 'What are you waiting for, eh? Help the negro! I promised Princess a brown baby to play with! Go on, wake her up!'

At least Princess is okay. What a relief.

One of the guys start slapping Pearl back into life, another pours a jug of cold water over her face. She comes round, all floppy and white-eyed, and tries to move, but they nail her down.

'Franz for you,' says Boss. 'He loves his hammers. *Make sure Franz isn't carrying any hammers*, I told Jett. You know how mantalicous Jett is, a pro, but Franz still managed to smuggle the hammer – inside of his left boot, of all places. It was just the right size to make a perfect hole in someone's head. Not too big, not too small, just right – like that story, Goldilocks, do you know it? Ahhh, this porridge is just right, yum-yum. Unacceptable behaviour, of course, attacking a mother-to-be with a hammer. But what can I do? Like I already stated, the boy loves his hammers.'

238

Jett. Where is he. Why isn't he here, saving lives. Like mine, for example. I could live. Seriously. I really could. No more pissing around, no more wastage. I mean it. I don't want to go down like this, not like this. So why isn't Jett saving me. Come on, God. Why isn't anyone coming to save me.

'So in the end, Jett failed me. Had to be punished – would you please excuse me for a just a second? Oi, morons! Can't you see she's bleeding to death? Mladen, put your hand on the wound, apply a steady pressure. Steady, I said! Franz, go get the First Aid kit from the truck, what are you gawping at me for, I said go!'

Punished. Punished how.

One… three… five… There are five men altogether, plus Boss. Two of them I know: Rob, the sadistic motherfucker who greeted me by running his finger across his throat, what a charming way to welcome a long lost friend, and young Blake, who keeps running to the veranda fence to throw up into the rhododendron bush Ivy often mistook for her dearly beloved. Rob's nose looks good, even better than the original version I managed to flatten after he had tortured Bella half to death. He ought to be grateful, really, not plot my demise. He also ought to have known better than beat the crap out of Charlotte, he just walked up to her and started to hit her, around the face, mostly, with his fists and elbows, then when she fell to the ground he continued to kick her again and again until suddenly he stopped, looked up at me and smiled. All I could do was stand there and watch, no one was holding me or anything, yet for some reason I just couldn't move. I know this will sound like the lamest of excuses, but it did feel like I was stuck in a middle of one of Pearl's giant *telarañas*, unable to move.

The other three men, Mladen, Franz and the anonymous one, they must be new. Keen as fuck. Trigger happy. And weirdly scarred, all along their arms and down their necks and faces, like tribesmen, except for the evident lack of honour. They also look dumb. Or have I mentioned this already. So dumb, in fact, I wouldn't be at all surprised to learn that those scars were accidently and repeatedly self-inflicted. What's Boss doing surrounding himself by all these stupid fucks. Miki may have been a psychopath, but he was also as shrewd as a snake, a peasant boy done well without ever losing the connections with his roots. These guys, I've seen their sort before. Rootless, ruthless small-time crooks you'll find crawling around every main coach station of any European capital. Twentieth century Artful Dodgers, always on the lookout for their next victim, always on the lookout for someone weaker to pounce on. Well I blame their mother. I blame their first grade teacher. I blame someone. Someone ought to pay.

Franz returns with the First Aid kit, and starts bandaging Pearl's head with a surprising yet visible expertise.

'Franz used to be a nurse,' says Boss.

'Doctor,' says Franz.

'What?'

'I was a doctor, Boss. Not a nurse.'

'Even better. Ay. Can you save her?'

'Yes, Boss, I believe I can.' He looks around. 'But those two, I'm not too sure.'

Boss waves his hand, like a fucking queen I always suspected him to be. 'Every great accomplishment carries a collateral. Hope you didn't get too attached, my little runt. Copenhagen syndrome, I read all about it. And then I knew, the only reason Igor isn't coming back to me, the only reason she's staying away is because she caught this terrible disease. But I'll get you better. Don't you worry, my girl, I'll get the spell out of you.' He leans in so close, I can smell his milky breath. 'I cried for you, you know. Every day, I cried and I cried, sometimes on the inside only, you know how it is with this lot, you show any sign of a weakness and they're on you like a pack of wolves.' So I was right. Bosses can't show their real feelings in front of their adoring public. And where is my gold star. 'You broke a grown man's heart, did you know that?' He grabs my shoulders. 'Did you? You broke my heart, Igor! I was doing fine without you, ay, I was doing great, but then you came along, you rose from that bloodied dust and saved my life, and I knew God sent you to me as a sign of his personal benediction. I took you under my wing, and I kept you warm and safe, I gave you all my tenderness – and still you leave me to rot all alone?' Boss lifts me off the ground and shakes me like a ragdoll. Bet he'll be sorry when my neck snaps. Not if, *when*. 'Have I not been merciful?' He throws me onto the ground, my head smashes against the tiles.

'Die, bitch!' Someone shouts.

But I don't die. I do far worse, I start to cry.

'What have I done?' Boss runs over and picks me up. 'I am so sorry! I didn't mean to hurt you, are you okay? Igor? Please tell me you're okay!' I nod into his hairy chest. Seriously. What's wrong with buttoning a shirt right up to the top. 'There, there, I won't let anything bad happen to you.' He gently rubs the back of my head. 'I am not like Jett.' Our eyes meet. 'Yes, yes, I know all about Jett. Seducing you like that, that dirty French bastard! Bet he told you all kinds of lies, ay, bet he told you he loved you more than I ever could. Brainwashed my little Igor into leaving me. Well he won't do that again in a hurry, or should I say he'll never do it again, not after the hundred lashings I gave him. I bought the whip especially, a proper horse whip from a farmer. Ripped him half to shreds, I did. See if the Hill People can use him as curtains, eh.'

Rob clears his throat.

'What?'

'Sorry Boss, it's only, well it's getting late, and I'm wondering what to do with the bodies… Burn them as per usual?'

Bodies. Jett. Curtains. And where the fuck is baby Godot when you need him the most.

'Go ahead, Rob.' Boss winks at me. 'So we can all go home.'

'What about this one?' Rob waves his hand towards me. 'I'd be more than happy to take care of her for you.'

'Take care of who?' Boss straightens up to his usual towering inferno. 'Do you mean Igor? Do you mean *my* Igor?'

'Yes, Boss, that's exactly who I mean.'

'If I were you, boy, I'd unmean it, and quick. Igor

is none of your business, the same goes for the rest of you lowlifes, is that clear?'

Rob clenches his fists. 'No offence, Boss, but this girl has committed a serious crime against my person, and she's murdered Miki, and on top of all that, she stole one of your best girls. I reckon she must pay for all the trouble she's caused. Eye for an eye, Boss – like you always say.'

'Who the hell you think you are, eh, quoting me like that?' Boss grabs Rob by the throat, and starts squeezing. 'You want Igor? You want my Igor? How dare you want my Igor?' Rob tries to say something, but all that comes out of his mouth is a raspy sound, very similar to the last squeal a pig makes after it's had its throat cut. I'm about to look away, the last thing I need right now is to see another evil dickhead get what's coming to him, when I spot a flash of the blade in Rob's hand. '*Boot!*' I shout.

But it's too late.

Boss's body crashes next to me with a mighty thump. The rest of the men point their guns at Rob.

'Easy,' Rob says. 'Easy now.'

Blake is the first to lower his gun. 'Fuck it.'

'Boss was losing the plot, you all saw it, right?' says Rob. 'He got what was coming to him, is all.'

The men exchange glances.

'He was obsessed with the runt,' says Rob. 'The man was *loco*.'

Somebody laughs. One by one, the men place their guns back into the holsters.

'Right then,' says Rob. 'Let's get this over and done with.'

'This one here…' Franz points at Pearl. 'Do you still want me to try and patch her up?'

Boss is staring at me like he's still in there. But I know he isn't. His eyes are switched off, like a blue lamp without a bulb. What if this was the only man who ever really loved me, what if he was the only man who ever would.

'Don't waste your talents, doc,' says Rob. 'She'll make a far better bonfire than she ever did a whore.'

The darkness rises from deep inside my belly. So sudden, so deep, it hits me like a hard ball of black. I yelp, and then I pounce.

I open my left eye, the right one is either on strike, or gone. I'm lying on my side, next to Boss who is still staring at me, gutter to stars style. If I strain my remaining eye as far up as it'll go, I can see:

a) Charlotte's feet, one shoe on, one shoe off, and

b) a glimpse of the great black night beyond.

I realise we're probably all dead by now. What a shitty fairy tale this one has turned out to be, think I's prefer a Disney version for just this once. A pair of boots appear, followed by another. Déjà vu. Or just another echo of another fucked up dream. I close my eye. And just as well that I do, because the next moment I'm covered in petrol, head to toes.

'Make sure they're soaked through!' The voice is muffled, but definitely Rob's. Didn't quite manage to murder him, then. What a shame. And does this mean that he won. What kind of world has Rob as a winner.

'Yes, Boss!' Oh come on. The real Boss is still at least lukewarm, dammit. Show some respect. 'Although… I think I saw Igor twitch.'

'Did you?' There's a pause. Why must there be a pause. Pauses make me nervous. I hold my breath. 'Must've been a trick of light.'

'Sure. No way she could've survived the thrashing you gave her.'

'Stupid little bitch, starting on me like that,' says Rob. 'Go on, burn her, burn them all!'

There is a clank of Zippo snapping open, then a scrape of metal against a flint. Perhaps they brought a faulty lighter. Perhaps it won't spark. My ears never worked this hard. The next moment, the terrace lights up as if bathed in midday sun. A woman screams, 'No!' The flame advances in yellow, orange and baby-blue spikes: it's pretty and it's spreading fast. The first person it reaches is Boss. I watch it lick him up and down like an overzealous porn kitten, I smell the scorched hair and hear the skin at the back of his neck crack, sizzle and pop. The white paint on the wooden fence lifts and buckles. Thin columns of black smoke rise up from the sleeves on Boss's navy-blue linen jacket. He was very fond of this jacket, kept it for special occasions. Guess it can't get any more special than your own death. Someone coughs. Mema used to make burnt toffee, said it was good for your throat. I loathed the taste. 'I'd rather choke to death than eat that!' I would say. 'I'd rather die, Mema, I really would!'

It's getting hot in here. I was never too good with heat. Give me a snowy peak anytime. Far too hot for Igor to handle. Time to close my little eye. Over and out.

There is a loud hissing sound in my ear that refuses to go away. Princess. She's come to save me. Slowly, slowly, I open my eye. Everything's covered in virgin snow. What kind of magic.

Someone lowers a fire extinguisher in front of my face.

'Careful. She'll need a stretcher.'

The fire extinguisher disappears. A pair of girl's legs take its place. They're bare and tanned and fine, like spring shoots on a young tree. I reach out and touch the delicate golden ankle bracelet with a spatter of single red roses loosely tied around the left ankle.

Well come on.

THE END

Made in the USA
Columbia, SC
23 January 2018